"As I'm sure you've
by nature."

"I hadn't noticed that at all."

Gwen put a hand on her hip and looked at him askance. "Come now. You couldn't possibly have missed my limp."

"Of course I noticed the limp, but that's not the same as being clumsy."

She looked as if she was weighing her words before she spoke. "You'll have to forgive me, Albert. I'm not used to anyone speaking so openly about my physical impairment."

"We all have challenges. Some are physical, some not as apparent to the eye." Albert shrugged, hoping to make her feel more at ease. "I choose my friends based on their personality and character, not on whether they can win at a foot race."

A deep laugh burst from Gwen and she put her hand flat against her stomach. "Oh dear, I'm certainly glad to hear that. Elsewise, you and I would have to part ways right now."

"That would be a terrible shame." He grinned, totally besotted by the charming, laughing woman in front of him.

Jennifer AlLee was born in Hollywood, California, and now lives in Las Vegas, Nevada, which just goes to show that God provides her with colorful surroundings. She has ten published books to her credit. When she's not spinning tales, she can be found playing tabletop games with friends, enjoying TV shows or movies and singing at the top of her lungs to whatever song happens to be playing.

JENNIFER AlLEE

A Worthy Suitor

HEARTSONG
PRESENTS

Recycling programs
for this product may
not exist in your area.

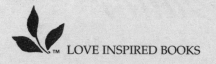 LOVE INSPIRED BOOKS

ISBN-13: 978-0-373-48779-0

A Worthy Suitor

www.Harlequin.com

Printed in U.S.A.

The Lord is my light and my salvation;
Whom shall I fear? The Lord is the strength
of my life; Of whom shall I be afraid?
—*Psalms* 27:1

To my mother, Rose-Marie, with all my love.

Chapter 1

Tuxedo Park, New York
June 1, 1901

Gwendolyn Banks was on the hunt. She moved through the trees, careful not to make unnecessary noise that might startle her quarry. The elusive zebra swallowtail butterfly had escaped her for the past few days, but it couldn't hide forever.

Not that the past few days had been fruitless. The book she clutched in her right hand was full of sketches and notations. Everywhere she looked, there was something new and wonderful to document. To Gwen's mind, it was impossible to be out amongst God's creation and not find something fascinating.

Gwen had been dismayed five years earlier when her father had announced his purchase of a vacation cottage in Tuxedo Park. In the exclusive community, there would be numerous opportunities to engage in cycling, tennis, dances and the like, all of which Gwen would need to find reasons not to be a part of. But when they arrived that first year, and Gwen discovered the treasure trove of natural wonders essentially in her own backyard, her thoughts on summer changed.

The chilled morning air seeped through the thin cotton of her walking suit, sending a shiver across her shoulders. Normally, she wouldn't be out quite this early, but she hoped the cool moistness would slow down the butterflies long enough for her not only to spot one, but to sketch it, as well.

A rustling sound caught her ear. Gwen stopped short, leaned against the nearest tree and peered around the trunk in the direction the noise came from. It was a man. He tromped through the foliage, a bow in his hand and a quiver of arrows slung over his shoulder. For one frivolous moment, Gwen let herself think about the romantic stories of Robin Hood, robbing from the rich and giving to the poor. But this wasn't one of the books she loved and she wasn't in Sherwood Forest. This was real life, and he was a very real man.

He was tall, his shoulders broad. He moved purposefully, threading through the trees as if he knew exactly what he sought. The man was obviously no stranger to the forest. A rabbit hopped into his path, then stopped, nose twitching, eyes round and bright as marbles. The man stopped as well and pulled an arrow from the quiver. Gwen's heartbeat quickened. Was he a hunter? She was fully aware where the meat on the dinner table came from, but she had no desire to witness the process that put it there.

Gwen watched as he positioned the arrow on the bow, then raised it, pulled back on the string and took aim. But he didn't aim at the rabbit, which now bounded away. Instead, he aimed at a thin tree. What in the world? Why would he shoot at a tree?

Then she saw it. There was the zebra swallowtail, its black-and-white-striped wings moving slowly together then apart, attempting to sun itself on the gray bark of the pawpaw tree. The color of the trunk combined with the slanted stripes of light and shadow cast through the leafy canopy provided effective camouflage for the butterfly. If Gwen hadn't been looking for it, she might have missed it. Did the archer see it?

If he did, he didn't care. With one eye squinted shut, he pulled farther back on the bow string until his thumb touched the underside of his jaw. He held his breath.

Before she could think twice, Gwen barreled forward.

"No! Stop!"

The man jerked and turned toward the sound of her voice as he let go of the string. The arrow whistled through the air, so close to Gwen's ear that she felt the rush of wind it created as it went by.

"Stop!" Now it was the man's turn to bellow out a warning, even though the arrow was already long gone.

Gwen tried to do as he said, but one foot caught on the other in a frustrating and all-too-familiar manner, and she fell to the ground in a heap. As she attempted to free herself from the tangle of her skirts, the man dropped his bow and moved to help her.

"I'm so sorry, Miss…" His voice trailed off as his eyebrows raised in a question.

"Gwendolyn Banks."

"Miss Banks. Albert Taylor, at your service."

He held out his hand, but Gwen frowned at him. "I wouldn't be in need of your service, Mr. Taylor, if you hadn't yelled at me."

The solicitous smile froze on his lips. "And I wouldn't have yelled at you if you hadn't put yourself in danger by running at a raised arrow." His eyes narrowed and he hunkered down beside her. "Why would you do such a reckless thing?"

She puffed out a frustrated sigh and pointed at the tree. "Because of the zebra—" It was gone.

"Did you say a zebra? You may have hit your head when you fell." He reached out to touch her forehead, but she pulled away.

"What? No, not a zebra. A zebra swallowtail. It's a butterfly, and it was right there on that tree you were aiming at."

"I know. That's what I was aiming at."

"I just said that."

He shook his head. "No, you said I aimed at the tree, but that's incorrect. I was aiming at the butterfly."

Gwen was so shocked, she couldn't formulate words. Her mouth moved silently until finally the questions burst out. "Why would you do that? Why would any sane person hunt a butterfly?"

"I assure you, I'm perfectly sane."

"Are you a lepidopterist?"

"A what?"

"A lepidopterist. A person who studies butterflies. And you obviously aren't one, or you'd know what it meant." She shook her head. "Of course you're not. That arrow would destroy the poor thing's body and make it less than worthless for pinning."

Mr. Taylor held up his hand to stop her now free-flowing words. "I instruct archery at the Tuxedo Park Clubhouse. I come out here to improve my aim."

"And you do that by shooting at butterflies?"

"I do that by shooting at the smallest target I can find. Today, that just happened to be a butterfly."

Gwen couldn't help wonder what would have happened to the rabbit if something smaller hadn't come along. "You must stop."

"Must I?"

The amusement in his voice brought heat surging to Gwen's cheeks. Mocking didn't sit well with her. "To kill these amazing creatures simply to improve your aim is nothing short of barbarous."

He winced and drew back just a bit. "I'm not a perfect man, but I assure you, my actions are far from barbarous." He rose to his feet and again held out his hand. "Now, please let me prove that my heart is not black by letting me assist you."

As much as she wanted to refuse his help, she knew it was foolish to do so. Struggling to her feet unaided would be unladylike and potentially humiliating. With a sniff she reached up and took his hand. Placing his other hand beneath her elbow, he pulled her up as if she weighed no more than the butterfly he'd almost impaled.

"Thank you."

"You are quite welcome, Miss Banks."

His lips quirked up in a smile, crinkling the corners of his eyes. She'd never met a man with eyes quite like his. They were a rich golden brown, like the topaz in one of Mother's many necklaces. But beyond their beauty, his eyes were compassionate and honest. Perhaps she had misjudged him.

"I apologize for my outburst, Mr. Taylor. I've been studying the flora and fauna here for the last five years. Some are easier to find than others, but the zebra swallowtail has been particularly difficult to observe. The thought that anyone would harm one simply to improve his aim, well, I find it appalling, to be perfectly honest."

He laughed and rubbed the back of his neck. "I doubt you've ever had a problem being honest."

"True." Gwen nodded. "Father says it's one of my worst faults."

"Not at all." Mr. Taylor shook his head. "I find honesty a virtue which is in short supply. It's refreshing to find someone who speaks her mind."

A ribbon of warmth wound its way through Gwen, even though she knew he was only being nice. He was a villager; she was a "Parkie." Of course he would be polite and considerate. Still, it was hard to imagine a man who spoke so highly of honesty would outright lie, so she let herself enjoy the compliment.

Shifting the quiver on his shoulder, he glanced at the tree and then back at Gwen. "It should please you to know that, even though I occasionally aim at butterflies, I've never hit one. They have a habit of flying away before the arrow gets close."

So he shot at them because he knew he wouldn't hit them. It was a strange thing to do, but she was glad he'd told her. The act of kindness was impressive. "I'm very pleased to hear that. Now if you'll excuse me, I must get home."

His eyes flickered downward, taking in the dirt smeared on the side of her skirt, then moved back up to her face. "Of course. Good day to you, Miss Banks."

She nodded. "Mr. Taylor."

How she wished he'd walk away so she could make her retreat in private. But it would be rude to turn one's back on a lady, so as she expected, Mr. Taylor stood watching her. Gwen turned with all the grace she could muster, praying that for once she could exit an encounter without eliciting pity. She took one step, then another, and then her secret was exposed.

Mr. Taylor hurried to her side, his fingers wrapping around her upper arm. "You're limping. You must let me help you."

"No, I'm fine. Really."

His expression plainly said that he didn't believe her. "No one walks that way when they're fine. You must have twisted your ankle."

"I assure you, there's nothing wrong with me that wasn't wrong when I left the cottage this morning." She hesitated, angry at the embarrassment she felt. "I was born with a deformity of the foot. That is the cause of the limp."

After spending her entire life dealing with people's reactions to her physical imperfection, Gwen had become quite adept at reading facial expressions. Most responded with pity. A few with revulsion. And a few with mean-spirited taunts. But the look on Mr. Taylor's face was altogether new. He was upset by his blunder, but he also emanated compassion. It was almost as if he understood what she was feeling.

His hand still on her arm, he looked her straight in the eye. "I'm glad that you weren't hurt by our meeting today. May I offer a word of advice?"

Oh, please, Lord, she prayed silently, *don't let him be a proponent of quackery.* But she smiled sweetly. "Certainly."

He leaned slightly forward and lowered his voice. "The next time you see someone like me out here, don't try to run in front of him."

Gwen put her palm flat over her heart and gasped in mock distress. "Oh no. You mean there are *more* like you?"

Albert Taylor's topaz eyes glimmered as he laughed deep and loud. "And again, a good day to you, miss."

His fingers left her arm, taking their warmth with them. Then he stepped away and moved to retrieve his errant arrow. Gwen forced herself to head in the other direction, back to the family cottage.

Many years earlier, she'd made a hard and fast rule not to indulge in flights of fancy where her heart was concerned. That's what books were for. In the pages of fiction, she could experience love and intimacy without having to deal with the pain of reality. But now, just for a moment, Gwen let herself imagine what it would be like to feel romantic love for someone who was flesh and blood.

Someone with eyes that sparkled like topaz.

It was much easier to locate an arrow when it hit its intended target than when it flew off course. Albert scanned the ground, moving aside low-growing plants with the end of his bow. On a normal day, he would have kept his eye on the shot and known exactly where the arrow went. But on a normal day, he wouldn't have been interrupted by a young lady determined to save the life of a zebra swallowtail.

Albert chuckled and shook his head. Her eyes had flashed when she took him to task for his choice of targets, and then, when she'd realized he wasn't intent on exterminating the butterfly population of Tuxedo Park, she'd offered a sincere apology. He'd met many social-ites during his years working at the club. Some treated him like a servant, while some flirted shamelessly as if it was a delightful summer game. Gwendolyn Banks was the first in recent memory, however, to treat him like a normal human being.

Something out of place caught his eye, and he turned to see the arrow's feathers sticking out from under a clump of weeds. Albert plucked it out triumphantly and slid it home into the quiver. Its loss wouldn't mean much to any of the Parkies, but to him, every arrow brought him one step closer to reaching his goal.

Albert turned on his heel. It was time to go to the club and prepare for another day of instructing the upper crust in the fine art of hitting a straw target. As he passed the pawpaw tree, he patted its trunk.

"Maybe tomorrow," he said. "But only if no butter-flies are around."

The toe of his shoe hit something, and he looked down. Half-buried under leaves was a book. Miss Banks must have dropped it when she fell. He picked it up, opened the leather cover and let out a long whistle. It was a sketchbook that had been transformed into a field journal.

With great care not to dirty it, he turned the pages, increasingly impressed. Some of the sketches were sim-ple, made with quick, black strokes, but others were ex-traordinary in their detail. A meticulously drawn bird of yellow and black looked as if it might fly off the page and escape into the trees.

Albert couldn't imagine the hours of work she must have put into her book. He had to return it to her, but how? He couldn't very well walk up to her family's cottage and rap on the door. No doubt she would come looking for it when she realized it was missing, so perhaps he should leave it where he'd found it. But the chance it would be ruined was far too great. The best thing would be to take it back to the clubhouse with him, and she could retrieve it there.

He flipped to the back of the book. At least one quarter of the pages were blank. He could use one to leave her a note in case she came back looking for her lost book, but he had nothing to write with. Now what?

Silently asking forgiveness for vandalizing her book, he tore out a page and headed back to the pawpaw tree. A smile lifted his lips. If Miss Banks was as bright as he thought she was, she'd understand his message, and he would see her again very soon.

Chapter 2

"Gwenie! Where have you been?"

Gwen smiled as her younger sister hurried down the walkway to meet her. "The same place I am most mornings—the woods."

Matilda stopped in front of her and pointed at Gwen's soiled skirt. "And this time, you've brought some of it home with you."

A flush heated Gwen's cheeks. "I had a little accident. But no harm was done."

"Save for your dress." Matilda sniffed. "I don't know what you find so fascinating out there. It's just the same old birds and trees and plants, over and over again."

"Oh, but you're wrong. Nature is ever changing." Gwen winked at her sister. "You'd see that if you took your eyes off the eligible dandies preening around the park."

Such a statement might offend another woman, but

not Matilda. Vivacious and full of life, she was fully aware that men circled around her like moons orbiting a planet. Her smile lit up her dark green eyes as she threaded her arm through the crook of Gwen's elbow. "Speaking of eligible dandies, why don't you come into town with me? Jason Adler has been boasting about his new motorcar, and he promised to take some of us for a ride."

"Mother won't let you go without me, will she?"

A frown tugged down the corners of her pretty mouth. "No. But I still would have asked you. It's always more fun with you along."

Oh yes, it was always more fun for Matilda to be tethered to her socially awkward, physically imperfect sister. Gwen forced down her sarcastic thoughts and reminded herself to be thankful. At times, she thought her sister was flighty and too concerned about superficial things, but at her core, Matilda was a sweet, loving girl.

Gwen tightened her arm around her sister's. "Of course I'll come with you. But I need to change first."

"Thank you, Gwenie." Matilda giggled with glee. "You'll see. Being amongst people is much better than traipsing around the woods by yourself."

Gwen allowed herself a secret smile. If she told her sister about the dashing archer she'd met today, Matilda would probably think she'd made him up. Perhaps Gwen needed to include a sketch of him in her field guide, just to prove his existence.

"Oh, dear." Gwen stopped short, jerking on Matilda's arm in the process.

"What's wrong? Is it your foot?"

Gwen frowned. Why was her foot always the first

thing anyone thought of? "No, it's my journal. I don't have it." She replayed the events of the morning in her mind: seeing the butterfly, charging at the man with the bow and arrow, falling down, his fingers wrapping around hers as he helped her up.

"I must have dropped it."

Matilda patted her arm and pulled her forward. "I'm sure Father will buy you a new one."

"I don't want a new one. I need *my* journal." She'd spilled her heart and soul onto the pages of that book. All the discoveries she'd made during hours and hours spent in the woods were recorded there. She had documented not just her findings in nature, but also things she'd discovered about herself. She couldn't possibly let it go without trying to find it.

They rounded a bend in the walkway and the family cottage came into view. Not for the first time, Gwen wondered why anyone would dub the elaborate mansions in Tuxedo Park *cottages*. Perhaps the founders had thought it sounded intimate and homey, but to Gwen, it was another example of the chasm between the classes. What the upper class considered a cottage was far and away beyond anything the villagers would ever live in.

Villagers like Albert Taylor.

As she trudged up the stairs to retrieve a clean dress and make herself presentable, Gwen made a decision. She'd accompany Matilda into town, but first, they had another stop to make.

"I don't understand why you had to bring me with you," Matilda grumbled as Gwen led her between the trees.

"I told you why." Gwen spoke to Matilda without looking at her. Even without her journal to sketch in, Gwen's eyes were keen, taking in every leaf, insect, bird and animal.

Matilda let out a little squeal, and Gwen finally looked back at her. She held her skirts high and stepped around a questionable mound of something on the forest floor. "Why couldn't you have gotten the silly book tomorrow without me?"

"Because it would be ruined by tomorrow." Gwen couldn't resist poking just a bit. "If the morning dew didn't soak the pages, the rodents would surely nibble away at them."

"Rodents?" Matilda's eyes widened as her voice lowered to a whisper.

Gwen nodded carelessly. "Squirrels, chipmunks, mice." She paused. "Rats."

"Goodness, let's find that book and get out of here." Matilda lifted her skirts higher and rose onto her tiptoes, as if less contact with the ground would make her less likely to encounter vermin.

"Yes, let's." Gwen chuckled as Matilda scuttled past her.

A few minutes later, they reached the place where Gwen had fallen. She examined the ground carefully, then sighed in dismay. "It's not here."

Matilda wrinkled her nose. "How do you know this is the right spot? It looks the same as everywhere else we've been."

"No, this is it. I recognize the fallen log there, and that clump of trillium there."

"What about that arrow over there?"

Gwen's head jerked up. "What?"

"Over there." Matilda pointed. "In that tree trunk."

Sure enough, there was an arrow, and something was pinned under it. Gwen's heart sank. What had that man done after she'd left? Pulling her shoulders back, she hurried to the tree, steeling herself for what she might find. But as she came closer, the worry in her heart lifted.

"What is it?" Matilda hadn't moved from her spot.

Beneath the arrow was a blank piece of paper. From the slightly jagged edge, it wasn't hard to tell where it had come from.

Rather than answer Matilda, Gwen pulled the arrow from the tree and folded the piece of paper into a neat square. "Come along, sister. We're going to town."

Matilda furrowed her brow in confusion. "But what about your book? Don't you care about it anymore?"

"Of course I do. And now I know exactly where to find it."

"The paper was blank. How could that tell you anything?" Matilda yanked her skirt away from the grasping fingers of a fallen tree branch and snorted in exasperation. "You owe me an explanation, Gwen."

Gwen laughed. For once, she knew something about a person in the park that her sister didn't, and she was enjoying it. "Just keep walking. It will all make sense eventually."

It didn't take long for them to reach the Tuxedo Park Clubhouse. Now they were in Matilda's domain, so Gwen let her take the lead. Her sister exchanged pleasantries with the people they passed, laughing and chatting. Gwen knew the ways of the natural world, but when it came to the ways of society, she yielded to Matilda's expertise.

Normally, Gwen went out of her way to avoid the clubhouse. Not that she was ashamed of her limp. She'd gotten used to the questioning looks and the occasional snicker behind a raised hand. But in truth, there had never been much there that interested her. Now, gazing out over the expanse of emerald green grass, the beds of meticulously kept flowers and shrubs surrounding the buildings and lining the walkways, and the blue-and-white excursion boats docked at the lake, Gwen began to reconsider the clubhouse's appeal. The flower beds alone were probably home to all manner of insects.

"Gwenie. I know that look." Matilda put a hand on her arm and whispered in her ear. "Don't you dare start poking around in the dirt."

Gwen laughed. "Don't worry, Tilda. I wouldn't dream of embarrassing you amongst your own kind."

Matilda looked at her askance, as if uncertain whether that statement was a compliment or an insult. "Thank you."

"Matilda!" A young man bounded up to them. His face was ruddy from excitement, and his hair the color and texture of straw stuck out from under a camel-colored driving cap.

"Hello, Jason." Matilda motioned to Gwen. "This is my sister, Gwendolyn. And this is Jason Adler."

"Pleasure to meet you, ma'am." His Adam's apple jerked up and down in his scrawny neck as he spoke, making him both awkward and likable at the same time.

Gwen nodded slightly. "Mr. Adler. A pleasure."

Jason turned to Matilda. "I'm taking Walter and Fay for a drive. Can you join us?"

She clapped her hands and gave a little jump. "I'd

love to." Then she looked at Gwen. "Will you be all right without me?"

"Of course I will. Contrary to what Mother tells you, I am perfectly comfortable on my own."

Matilda smiled, relief relaxing her features. "Thank you."

With a wave of her hand, Gwen dismissed her. "You go have fun. I'll be at the archery range."

The look on Matilda's face said that she expected the full story, with details, upon her return. Jason put a hand on her elbow and led her forward. When they'd moved a few steps away, he tilted his head toward Matilda's ear.

"I didn't even know you had a sister."

The remark shouldn't have hurt. Neither should have Matilda's laughter in response. But they both did. It was Gwen's own fault, really. She'd isolated herself, content to be alone with nonjudgmental woodland creatures and silent plant life. There was no reason for Matilda to mention her sister to her friends, because Gwen was never around to meet any of them.

Shoulders back, spine straight as a marble column, Gwen walked forward. Two boys, about ten years of age, ran past her, laughing and shouting. One looked over his shoulder and pointed in her direction. The other one punched him in the arm and they both laughed harder. Gwen watched them running until they were too far away to see anymore.

She blinked hard, refusing to give in to the tears that burned her eyes. There was no way to know what they were laughing at. It may not have been her. But Gwen always assumed she was the butt of the joke.

It had been a mistake to send Matilda off. Despite what she'd said to her sister, Gwen really didn't feel comfortable by herself. Without her sister to draw people's attention like metal shavings to a magnet, Gwen was more exposed than ever. So many people. So many chances to make a fool of herself. She stood out in the open, her feet frozen to the ground.

Eyes closed, Gwen offered up a silent prayer. *Help me to move, Lord. Help me not to care what others think. Give me courage.*

"Miss Banks?"   ·

Her eyelids snapped open. Albert Taylor stood before her, his gaze warm and bright, smile dazzling. Was this how God had chosen to answer her prayer? If so, it was the quickest, most pleasant answer she'd ever received.

"Mr. Taylor. I was just about to go looking for you."

"I'm glad I saved you the trouble."

Trying to keep her voice steady proved difficult, mostly because of the way her heart was fluttering away in her chest. "I believe you have something of mine."

"Yes, I do. And you have something of mine." He pointed to the arrow she held clutched in her hand, pressed against the side of her skirt.

She held it out to him with the point facing downward. "That was a clever note you left for me. Like a treasure map written in invisible ink."

He ducked his head, then looked back at her with a grin as he took the arrow. "I hope you'll forgive me for tearing a page out of your book, but it was the only thing I could think to do. I'm not in the habit of carrying a pen and ink around with me."

"There's nothing to forgive. I'm just so pleased you found my journal." She looked at his hands, but he held nothing. "Where is it?"

"In a safe place on the archery range."

She looked over his shoulder. In the distance, she saw several men and two women aiming arrows at large, round targets on wooden stands. "I've never visited the archery range."

His brows lifted in surprise. "Then we must remedy that immediately." He offered his elbow. "Would you allow me the honor of escorting you?"

Gwen didn't know how to respond. All around them, couples walked together in the same manner he suggested. She would be much less conspicuous on the arm of a gentleman. And it might be her only chance to have such an experience, even if it was only being offered out of consideration. "Yes. Thank you, sir."

She put her arm through his, and as he smiled down on her, she told herself that those sparkling eyes had nothing to do with her decision.

Miss Banks had been terrified. She'd never admit it, and Albert would never embarrass her by pointing it out. But as soon as her sister left her side, her confidence left her, too.

He'd spotted them from the archery range and watched as young Mr. Adler pulled the sister away. She'd seemed fine at first, but then the boys ran past her, and he could see her defenses crumbling. She couldn't know they'd actually been laughing at a fellow who'd fallen off a bicycle while trying to impress a girl. Miss Banks had heard the laughter, and immediately decided it was at her expense.

Albert knew all too well what it was like to feel that every critical eye was cast upon you, and he couldn't leave her standing alone. Now, as they walked together to the target area, he kept his pace slow and his arm rigid, giving her something to balance on if need be.

"I found your field journal fascinating, Miss Banks."

She looked up at him, her face transformed by a brilliant smile. "Thank you. And please, my friends call me Gwen." Her eyes darted away. "After rescuing my journal, I consider you my friend."

Albert puffed his chest out just a bit. "Thank you, Gwen. You have quite a talent. The drawings are impressive."

Gwen laughed. "Only because you didn't see my early attempts. When I first started drawing, everything looked the same. You couldn't tell a cricket from a grasshopper from a praying mantis."

"I must say, I've never met a woman who was so comfortable with bugs." She turned her head away, and Albert knew she'd misinterpreted his comment. "I mean that as a compliment."

She nodded without looking at him, the change in her demeanor was unmistakable.

"Here we are." He stopped at the edge of the archery range. "I'll get your book. Can I trust you to stay here and not run in front of any arrows?"

She tried unsuccessfully to hold back a smile. "As long as no butterflies are in danger, I won't budge from this spot."

"Good."

Albert jogged to a locked case in which he kept his personal items. He took out the journal and started to shut the lid, but then he stopped. He could return her journal, in which case Gwen would go home and their encounter would be over. He thought back to the confident woman he'd met in the woods, and how different her demeanor was when surrounded by people. She needed to interact with people in a way that would shore up her confidence. He put the journal back in the case and took out his bow and arrow. This just might be the way.

Chapter 3

Gwen stood on the outskirts of the archery range, hands clasped tightly in front of her. If she wished very hard, perhaps she could blend into the background like the elusive zebra swallowtail. Thankfully, the people around her were so absorbed in their own activities no one seemed to notice her or her anxiety.

"Here you are, safe and sound." Mr. Taylor jogged up to her, smiling warmly.

Relief at no longer being alone washed over Gwen in a wave. "Yes, I was able to stay out of trouble. But it appears you forgot something."

At his frown she looked from his one hand, which held a bow, to the other, which held a quiver of arrows. Her journal was nowhere to be seen.

"Ah, yes." He nodded and his eyes sparkled with the secret he was about to reveal. "It occurred to me that, since you shared your love of nature with me, although quite accidentally, it's only right that I share what I love with you."

Gwen's chest tightened. "Archery?"

"Yes." He hoisted his full hands a bit higher.

For years, Gwen had spent her summers avoiding the various sporting activities available at Tuxedo Park. Swimming was too revealing. Tennis required too much coordination. Cycling was downright painful. But archery? She'd never considered it.

Looking at the row of male and female archers standing across from straw targets, her heart skipped a bit. Other than maintaining a steady stance, success seemed dependent on the arms and torso. She might actually be able to do this.

"I would enjoy that, Mr. Taylor."

He looked at her askance. "Really, Gwen? Do you call all your friends by their surnames?"

The warmth of a blush crept across her cheeks. "Now that you mention it, no, I don't. I would enjoy an archery lesson, *Albert*."

"Excellent."

He led her to the nearest open space, which was several hundred feet away from the targets. Gwen balked and shook her head. "Do we have to start so far away from them?"

Albert chuckled. "The arrows fly farther than you expect. Don't worry. Eventually, this will seem perfectly normal."

He explained the equipment to her. She learned that the feathers on the back of the arrow aided in balance and direction. The indent at the back was a nock. When that indent was placed against the bowstring, it was called nocking the arrow.

"You need a good foundation, so plant your feet firmly. Like this." Albert stood sideways, his right foot braced behind him and his left forward and pointing at the target.

Gwen maneuvered herself into the same position, thankful that, although he watched her progress, he never once asked if her foot made it difficult. It was amazing the things people assumed she couldn't do just because of her damaged foot.

When she was satisfied with her progress, she looked up at Albert expectantly.

"Excellent. Now on to the bow."

He demonstrated how to hold it, and then he handed it to her. She wrapped the fingers of her left hand around the grip, noting the warmth that lingered from his hand.

"Not quite there. A little higher."

Before she knew what was happening, he moved her hand up on the bow and folded her fingers down. For a moment, his hand completely covered hers, and for that same moment, Gwen forgot how to breathe.

"There now, that's better."

Brought back to earth by Albert's businesslike attitude, Gwen forced herself to concentrate on properly nocking the arrow. It was much harder than it looked. As she pulled back on the bowstring, the arrow rose out of position and off the arrow rest, first pointing to the sky and then falling so far down that it aimed at the ground. Gwen bit her lip, trying unsuccessfully to hold back a growl of frustration.

Albert chuckled. "That's exactly how I felt the first time I did this. Try to relax."

That was easy for him to say. She dropped her arms, took a deep breath and started again. Bow up. Arrow aligned. With a finger above and below the notch, she pulled back on the string while trying to hold the arrow in place. This time, it fell out of her grasp completely and landed at her feet.

"This is pointless." Gwen shook her head in frustration. One more sport, one more failure. She should have known better than to try.

Albert picked up the arrow and held it out to her. "It's far too soon for giving up. Try again."

She had two choices: walk away or do as he said. Walking away alone would expose her to further ridicule, but even worse, she didn't want to run the risk of insulting Albert. He'd been nothing but kind to her. For some reason, she felt safe with him, as though he would shield her from the thoughtless remarks and rude glances that often came her way. She couldn't give up yet.

"What am I doing wrong?"

"You're tensing up and making your grip too tight." He began to reach for her hand, then paused as if thinking better of the idea. "May I show you?"

He was going to touch her again. "Yes, please." Gwen forced the words past the lump in her throat.

Albert moved behind her, shadowing her stance. His left arm followed hers, adjusting her grip on the bow. He bent his body enough so that his mouth was close to her ear as he spoke. "Don't pinch the string between your fingers. Let it lay in the crease behind your knuckles. Like this."

When her fingers were where they belonged, his hand moved to her wrist and pulled gently back until the arrow's feathers grazed her cheek. He stepped away, taking his warmth with him and leaving her momentarily bereft. But then she realized she was holding the bow on her own. She had the string pulled back, the arrow exactly where it should be and the target was in sight. This was her moment. "Now?" she whispered.

"Now."

The arrow sailed through the air. It went high, then arced down as it neared the target, then pierced the canvas-covered straw with a thump. It was the outer ring of the target, but she had hit it.

"I did it!" She hoisted the bow in the air and turned with such exuberance that she almost hit him in the face with it.

"Yes, you most certainly did." Albert smiled warmly. "I must say, I'm impressed. Most people don't hit the target their first time out."

"Truly?" Gwen put her free hand to her chest. "You're not just saying that to make me feel good, are you?"

Albert's expression turned serious. "I assure you, I would never say something for such a shallow reason. Pandering does no one any good."

Oh, dear. Now she had insulted him. "Albert, I'm sorry. It's just...I'm so used to people treating me like I'm made of glass. This—" she motioned toward the target, then back at him "—and your compliment, well, today has been an altogether new experience for me."

The smile returned to his lips. "And a good experience, I hope."

"Fabulous."

"Then I expect to see you again. My schedule is

posted in the clubhouse, but if you want a lesson at a different time, I'll do my best to accommodate you."

Reality splashed Gwen, cold and fast. Of course, he was a teacher. The interest he showed in her was nothing more than a ploy to take on another paying customer. How silly she had been to attribute his kindness to anything else.

If she was smart, she would go back to her field studies and avoid the clubhouse like she always had. Still, she couldn't deny the strength she'd felt as she pulled back on the bowstring, or the rush of adrenaline that shot through her when she released the arrow. But she had to keep her head. She had to remember that no matter what kind of attraction she might feel for Albert, there was no way he would return those feelings. Even if the class difference wasn't an issue, which it always was, a man like him would never be interested in someone like her.

As long as she kept the facts foremost in her mind, she would be able to guard her heart. Albert Taylor was a teacher, and she had just decided to become a student of archery.

"Oh yes," she said with a decisive nod. "You will most definitely see me again."

Matilda's unending chatter about the virtues of young Mr. Adler made the walk home feel interminable.

"He's such a talented driver. A dog ran right in front of the automobile, and he was able to swerve to miss it."

"That is quite an accomplishment." Gwen didn't bother adding that drivers were required to move at such a snail's pace within the park that it would be far more difficult to hit a moving target than to miss one.

Matilda looked at her sister with a frown. "I'm sorry. Here I am going on and on about my lovely time, and I haven't even asked about yours. I see you retrieved your notebook."

"Yes, I did." Gwen pressed the journal more firmly against her chest. After promising Albert she would return the next afternoon for a proper lesson, he had fetched it from his locker and returned it to her.

"And what did you do with yourself after that? Oh, dear." She linked her arm around Gwen's and hugged her tightly to her side. "I hope you weren't too bored waiting for me."

Gwen smiled to herself. Of course her sister would assume that she'd had to content herself with watching others go about their business. She should shock Matilda by telling her that she'd amused herself by digging in the flower beds and tracing the movements of the common earthworm. On the other hand, Matilda would likely find the truth much more shocking.

"I wasn't bored at all. In fact, I spent quite a pleasant hour on the archery range."

Matilda stopped so suddenly, she almost threw Gwen off balance. "You? You took part in a sport?"

Gwen pulled her arm away from her sister and did her best to look indignant. "Why is that so shocking?"

"Because you loathe sports. You've done everything a person can think of to avoid them every summer."

"That's true." Gwen continued walking at a leisurely pace toward home. Even though she'd decided to be realistic about her interactions with Albert, that didn't mean she couldn't have a little fun with her sister. "But Albert convinced me that I might enjoy archery. And he was right."

"Albert?" Matilda hustled ahead of Gwen, stopping in front of her and bringing them both to a halt. "You've only just met the man, and already you're calling him by his first name?"

"I may have just met him, but he's spoken to me more than any other man has during the course of an entire summer."

"Oh no." Matilda hung her head, then looked back up at her sister. "Please tell me you haven't developed an infatuation for this man."

Gwen's cheeks burned. "Don't be absurd. He rescued my field journal and was kind to me, so I consider him a friend. That's all."

"But he's a villager."

"What difference does that make? He's a human being, worth just as much in the eyes of God as you and I are."

Matilda rolled her eyes to the sky. "That's not what I meant, and you know it. I think the whole class system is ridiculous. But Father doesn't. And we both know he would never bless a romance between you and a villager."

"Tilda, you are spinning fanciful tales where none exist. Albert is going to instruct me in the sport of archery, nothing more." She lifted her chin and pulled back her shoulders. "Now, let us go home before Mother sends out a search party."

They walked the rest of the way in silence. Despite her protests and her determination to remember that Albert was her teacher and nothing more, Gwen couldn't deny the thrill of Albert's hand on hers as he helped her with the bow, and the warmth that shot through her when he smiled. No, if she was truthful with herself, she had to admit having an attraction to the handsome archery instructor. But it was only a harmless crush. After all, no matter how she felt about him, he couldn't possibly be interested in her as anything more than a student and perhaps a friend. But that didn't dampen the excitement that coiled within her. For once in her life, the summer promised to include more than just long hours alone in the woods with the flora and fauna.

They turned the corner and started up the long driveway to the house. Father sat in a wide wicker chair on the veranda, as he did every afternoon, his summer suit neatly pressed but spotted with water droplets from the glass of iced lemonade he held in one hand. But this time, he wasn't alone.

Matilda nudged Gwen in the ribs with her elbow. "Who do you suppose that is?"

"I have no idea." Gwen squinted to get a better look. The man didn't seem at all familiar. He was engaged in a lively conversation with her father, leaning forward in his seat, obviously engrossed in the older man's words.

She was just wondering if they should call out and make their presence known when Father turned to look their way.

"Ah, there you are, Gwen." His booming voice carried quickly down the long driveway. "There's someone I'd like you to meet."

A sneaking suspicion began to grow in Gwen as they drew closer. Father and the man stood. The stranger's eyes immediately went to Matilda, but then he pulled them away and looked at Gwen. His lips curled up into a stiff smile as she climbed the stairs.

Father motioned between her and the man. "Charles, this is my eldest daughter, Gwendolyn. And this is Mr.

Charles Drexler. He's one of the brightest stars at the brokerage firm. I thought the two of you might hit it off." He punctuated his words with the slightest of winks in Gwen's direction.

Gwen's heart dropped even as she reached out to take Mr. Drexler's extended hand. Just when her summer was beginning to look up, Father had to decide to play cupid. He'd done it before, trying to arrange matches between her and any number of eligible young men. She'd had nothing in common with any of them, and had asked Father to stop. But now he'd brought her one of his employees, and to their summer home, no less. She had the unpleasant task of finding a respectful way to let Father know the only arrows she was interested in were the ones she'd be shooting on the archery field with Albert Taylor.

Chapter 4

Gwen rested her fork gently against the china plate, afraid that making any noise would draw attention back to her. She really needn't worry. Since Matilda had discovered that Charles Drexler was being groomed by her father for bigger things at the firm, she had become overly animated, even for her.

"Is this your first visit to Tuxedo Park, Mr. Drexler?" Matilda leaned so far forward, it brought her bodice precariously close to her dinner plate.

"Yes, it is." Charles nodded politely. "I've heard a great deal about the activities that abound here."

Gwen lifted her water goblet to her lips as her mind drifted back to the archery range.

Father speared a thick pork chop from the serving plate in the middle of the table and dropped it unceremoniously on his plate. "It's high time you experience some of the finer things in life, young man." He looked across the table at his wife. "Which is why I've invited Charles to spend the next month here with us."

Gwen gasped, sucking water into her windpipe, which immediately produced a most unladylike coughing fit.

Charles's eyes narrowed in concern. "Are you all right, Miss Banks?"

Her mother and Matilda both held napkins out to her at the same time. Matilda smiled sweetly at Charles. "She'll be fine. This kind of thing happens all the time."

Bristling slightly at Matilda's cavalier attitude about Gwen's proclivity for embarrassing herself, she managed to shoo away the offered napkins and stop coughing. "I'm fine," she rasped.

Her father continued on as if nothing had interrupted him. "Charles was concerned about a month of not working, but since I own the company, that really isn't a problem." He laughed, then pointed his empty fork toward the ceiling. "We've got the guest quarters in the East wing going empty. Might as well use them."

He and Mother began talking about arrangements, and Matilda excitedly told Charles what he could expect in Tuxedo Park.

"Oh, you'll have so much fun. There are parties, and picnics. And a sweet little ice cream shop that makes the best sundaes you've ever had. Oh, and tomorrow, we'll take you to the clubhouse and introduce you to everyone, won't we, Gwen?"

"Of course." Gwen forced herself to remain calm, but she really wanted to yell at her sister to mind her own business. Gwen had, in fact, planned on visiting the clubhouse the next day, but not in order to give a newcomer a tour. She had a lesson with Albert, and she had no desire for company. As Matilda twittered on, a plan began to form in Gwen's head. Having company upon her arrival at the clubhouse might be a good thing. It would draw people's attention away from her. With a little persuasion, her sister might be amenable to distracting Charles and introducing him to her circle of friends while Gwen had her lesson.

"That's a wonderful idea, Tilda," Gwen said with a smile. "But you know everyone there is to know at the clubhouse, much more so than I. We will have to depend on you to be our main source of information."

Matilda beamed at her sister, her chest so swelled with pride Gwen feared one of her pearl buttons might pop off and fly across the room.

Gwen looked down at her plate to hide her satisfied grin. Yes, Matilda would need very little persuasion, indeed.

Some people refused to take instruction.

Albert stood back, arms crossed over his chest, as he watched the dandy at the firing line manhandle an arrow onto the bow. Lawrence Simmons seemed to think his status as the heir to the Simmons manufacturing fortune meant he was automatically good at everything he tried. If it hadn't been for the club's requirement of at least one lesson before a patron was allowed to shoot on the field, Albert had no doubt the arrogant young man would have forgone lessons entirely. Still, it was Albert's job to at least try to help.

"If you loosen up on the grip—"

"I've got this." Lawrence growled as he pulled back

on the bowstring, bringing it past his ear, which stuck out from his head at a decidedly prominent angle.

Albert took a step forward. "You really don't want to do that."

Lawrence's brows furrowed in concentration and a moment later he let go of the string. Rather than the satisfying pluck and hum he was used to, Albert heard a muffled thump as the string hit Lawrence's ear. It was followed by something akin to the wail of a cat whose tail had just been stepped on. Lawrence dropped the bow and stumbled backward, holding his palm against the side of his face.

"The whole idea of lessons is to keep me from being injured." Lawrence turned to Albert. "I'm going to report you to the director."

It was all Albert could do to hold back the retort on his tongue. "Sir, I attempted to correct your stance, your hold on the bow and its proximity to your face. If you would like to inform the activities director that you ignored all my recommendations and then hurt yourself, I can't stop you. But I should let you know, the clubhouse has a long and complex grapevine. It won't take long before the whole place is talking about the status of your ear."

The idea that any attention would be brought to his ears was apparently enough to make Lawrence rethink his complaint. With a huff, he dropped the bow on the ground. "This is a silly game anyway. I've got better ways to spend my summer."

As the injured man stalked away, Jonah Walker approached Albert.

"I see you charmed another student." Jonah laughed as he clapped Albert on the back.

Albert frowned. "He was unpleasant, but I hate to lose anyone."

"If we don't teach, we don't eat, eh?" Jonah nodded his understanding. "I remind myself of that every time the Golden Boy steps up to the line."

Albert laughed. Jonah had taken to giving his students nicknames that he used only when talking to other instructors. There was Lady Athena, a young woman with the unfortunate name of Gladys Crump, who was as fierce with a bow as she was lovely to look at; and there was Brandon Farthingham, also known as the Golden Boy, a man with enough money and status to be thoroughly annoying, but with enough true skill and desire to learn that Jonah couldn't help but tolerate him.

"At least Mr. Farthingham listens to your instruction." Albert shook his head. "Mr. Simmons believes himself much too good for that."

Jonah waved his hand as though shooing away a fly. "Enough about him. It looks as if your fortune is about to change." He motioned down the field with a nod of his head.

Albert's heart took an unexpected leap at the sight of Gwendolyn Banks moving in his direction. He'd seen her name on his teaching schedule for the day, but part of him had been sure something would happen to keep her from showing up. Yet there she was. Dressed in a practical day dress of sage green that set off the auburn highlights in her hair, she walked with her eyes focused on the ground. It was likely she was looking for uneven spots to avoid tripping, but he suspected her eyes were down to avoid looking at others. He wanted to tell her how she outshone the other ladies in their fancy dresses of white lace and ruffles. Instead, he lifted his hand in a greeting.

"Good to see you, Gwen."

Her head snapped up, and a smile immediately transformed her features. "Hello, Albert."

"Yes, hello." A fellow Albert hadn't noticed walked up beside Gwen, the scowl on his face indicating a proprietary expectation.

Gwen's sister, Matilda, hurried up on the other side of the man and stopped just short of grabbing his arm. If Gwen noticed, she cared not a whit.

"Albert, this is Mr. Charles Drexler." She inclined her head in the man's direction. "He's a business associate of our father."

Albert extended his hand in greeting, but Charles replied with a curt nod, then looked Albert up and down critically. "And you, sir?"

A slight scowl pulled down Gwen's brows, but she quickly replaced it with a placid expression. "Albert is my archery instructor."

"Archery?" Charles jerked his head back in surprise. "Why ever would you waste your time with such a frivolous pursuit?"

Albert barely refrained from rolling his eyes heavenward. Another parkie who had no idea of the nuances of the sport. How he wanted to put a bow in the man's hand and prove just how difficult it really was. Instead, he put on a pleasant face. "Archery isn't for everyone, but I'd hardly call it frivolous."

Gwen nodded her agreement. "It's a fascinating combination of athleticism, balance and concentration. I find it quite challenging."

"Of course you do." Charles smiled indulgently, then

turned to Matilda. "Are you as enthralled by this game as your sister is?"

Matilda's nose wrinkled as she pursed her lips. "Heavens no. There are so many more interesting things to do in the park."

"What a wonderful idea." Gwen clapped her hands together in what Albert was certain was an overexaggerated act of enthusiasm. "There's no need for the two of you to stand around here while I take my lesson. Tilda, why don't you show Charles around and introduce him to your friends?"

For the first time, Charles looked interested in the subject at hand. "A fabulous suggestion."

A coy smile brought out the dimples in Matilda's cheeks and her lashes fluttered. "It would be my pleasure. That is, if Charles doesn't mind."

"My dear lady, I would greatly enjoy having you as my guide." He bent his arm, offering her the crook of his elbow.

The younger Banks girl simpered as she threaded her arm through his and they began to walk away. Three steps later, Matilda pulled him up short and looked over her shoulder. "Gwenie, are you certain you don't mind us leaving you?"

"Of course not. You have fun. I want to hear all about it over dinner tonight."

"Dinner?" Matilda tilted her head. "Aren't you walking back home with us?"

Gwen shook her head. "I have something to tend to after my lesson."

"I'm not sure I can agree with that, miss." Charles frowned. "Your father left you in my charge. I'm responsible for you."

Two twin roses bloomed in Gwen's cheeks, and Albert could see her struggle to temper her response. "I appreciate your concern, Mr. Drexler. But I assure you, I am perfectly capable of taking care of myself. You have no responsibility for my welfare."

Matilda laughed, unaffected by the tension of the moment. "Oh, yes, Gwenie spends every summer traipsing all over Tuxedo Park on her own. I dare say, she knows the place better than the locals. Oh, look!" Matilda pointed with her free hand. "There's Jason. Maybe we can convince him to give us a ride in his automobile."

Before Charles could say another word, Matilda was tugging him across the field. "See you at dinner, Gwenie!" she called back over her shoulder.

Gwen chuckled to herself. "From time to time, my sister's joie de vivre comes in handy."

Albert laughed. "I take it that means you wanted them to leave."

"Of course. How else could I concentrate on my lesson?" Gwen clapped her hands together and grinned broadly. "Shall we get to it?"

The joy on her face reminded Albert of a child ready to open presents on Christmas morning. This was the reason he loved to teach, and something he saw very little of in the bored, rich patrons of Tuxedo Park. Gwendolyn Banks was like a refreshing breeze on a warm summer day. For the next hour, he intended to forget the annoyances of work and the troubles at home. For now, he wanted to share in the joy this lovely young woman radiated.

"By all means," he said, sweeping his hand in the direction of the targets. "Let us begin."

* * *

Gwen had always considered evening meals deadly dull, but they were even more so now that Charles Drexler was part of the conversation. In the past, Father would drone on about politics and business, with only his wife and daughters to listen and nod at appropriate times. But now, Charles was there to throw in his opinions, which invariably mirrored those of his employer. Gwen began to wonder if Charles was capable of forming individual thoughts, or if his views had to be spoon-fed to him through others.

"If you ask me, Roosevelt's wasting his time as vice president. It's an ineffectual, figurehead position. He'd have been able to do much more good if he'd stayed governor." Father cut his meat with so much gusto, Gwen feared he might saw straight through the plate.

"You're absolutely right, sir." Charles nodded and picked up his water goblet as if toasting Father. "I couldn't agree more."

"There's a surprise," Gwen muttered under her breath.

"What was that, Gwen?" Father's frown indicated she may not have spoken as quietly as she thought.

"I'm surprised that Tilda hasn't told us more about her time at the clubhouse today." She turned her attention quickly to her sister. "Were you able to coerce Jason to take you for a drive in the motorcar?"

Matilda's mouth turned down into a frown. "No. I'm afraid there was a bit of an accident yesterday, so Jason has been banned from driving for the foreseeable future."

Mother looked up from her plate in concern. "Oh, dear. I hope no one was hurt."

"Only Mrs. Jepson's prizewinning roses." Matilda

tried unsuccessfully to hold back a giggle. "I heard he plowed straight through them and rested the car on the Jepsons' porch."

The image was difficult for Gwen to comprehend. As slowly as Jason usually drove, he should have been able to avoid any target, much less one that was planted in place.

"That's a shame," Gwen said. "What did you do, then?"

"Well, I showed Charles around the grounds and introduced him to everyone. Oh, and we ran into Eloise Kane, and she said her parents are throwing a grand party next week." She clasped her fingers around her mother's wrist and squeezed. "Isn't that fabulous? We can go, can't we?"

"I don't see why not." She looked at her husband. "What do you think, Reginald?"

Mr. Banks nodded heartily as he finished chewing and swallowed. "I think it would be the perfect opportunity for these two youngsters to step out and announce their intentions."

Gwen's fork paused in midair, and she looked from her father to Charles. "Which two youngsters? You and Matilda?"

"What? Oh, no." Charles stammered his answer. "I mean, Matilda is a beautiful young woman but, well…"

"But what?" Matilda's voice rose in high-pitched indignation.

Mr. Banks held his hands up to quiet them all down. "Don't worry, Gwen, I brought Charles home for you, not your sister. Heaven knows she does well enough on her own." The words pierced Gwen's heart, but her father continued on without noticing. "I do believe someone is displaying a bit of jealousy, eh, Charles?"

Jealousy, indeed. More like ire at the idea that her father would bring someone home for her because she wasn't woman enough to attract a man on her own. As if having a man, any man, at her side was the be-all and end-all of her existence. And what did Charles think of all this? One look at the scowl on his face and the way he squirmed in his chair told her he wasn't a fan of the idea, but he wasn't about to contradict her father, either.

With great deliberateness, Gwen lifted the napkin from her lap, folded it and placed it gently on the table beside her plate. Then she pushed back her chair and slowly stood. "If you'll all excuse me, I would like to take leave of this conversation."

Mother blanched. "But, dear, the meal isn't over. We still have a lovely shortcake for dessert."

"Really, Mother, I'm afraid I couldn't eat another bite." In fact, she was having difficulty keeping down the food she'd already eaten. She gave Charles a pointed look. "Enjoy the rest of your evening."

Low, nearly whispered conversation followed her as she left the dining room and made her way up to her bedroom. Later, she would need to have a conversation with Father, and she'd most certainly need to talk to Charles, as well. For now, all she wanted was the company of a good book. With a little luck, she could disappear into another world, a world far from social conventions, class structure and meddling parents.

And if she happened to pick up *Robin Hood*, and read about the adventures of the dashing archer who roamed through Sherwood Forest, well, what was the harm in that?

Chapter 5

Albert trudged up the road. The more distance he put between himself and the country club, the more tired he became. It really should be the other way around. Heading home after an honest day's work should make a man happy and invigorated. But all Albert could think about was what might be waiting for him.

His home was a small hovel in a row of nearly identical small hovels that housed most of the people who worked in the tony community of Tuxedo Park. It was less than a mile from the gated and walled community, but it might as well be in a different country. Still, it was home. He didn't have a lot of money, but he kept it as nice as he could. And he had dreams. Dreams of something better, something where he could provide for his family without having to kowtow to the rich and pompous. Unfortunately, the only way those dreams could come true was by taking advantage of the connections he currently had in Tuxedo Park. It was a vicious cycle, but one he hoped to break out of as soon as possible.

As his boots crunched on the gravel walkway, a movement caught his eye. He looked at the front window just in time to see the curtain fall back into place. He frowned and muttered under his breath. How many times had he told Rachel not to wait for him at the window? If anyone found out about his sister, the consequences could be catastrophic.

Despite his frustration, he made sure he was smiling when he walked through the door. Her mood swayed wildly of its own accord, but one frown from him could send her into a depression that might last for days. He found her in the front room, sitting in her favorite chair, hunched over her needlework.

"Hello, *liebling*." His German mother had always said the word meant *sweetheart*, which was what he'd told Rachel it meant. Frankly, Albert didn't really care how it was translated. Saying it made him feel closer to his mother. If she were still alive, she'd have some strong words for him, of that he was certain.

"Albert, you're finally home!" Rachel jumped to her feet and ran to him. In the process, the hooped canvas fell to the ground, landing beside her sewing box.

He braced himself as she jumped into his arms, then laughed as she knocked half the air from his lungs. No matter what she did, he couldn't stay upset with her for long. It had been that way since they were children and she followed him around like a loyal puppy dog.

He hugged her tightly and cupped the back of her head with his hand. He found a rat's nest of a knot near the base of her skull, and his heart sank. For a knot like that to develop, she hadn't brushed her hair in days. How could he have missed it? He'd been so preoccupied with his work, his own ambitions. And then there was Gwen. She was so unlike most of the snobby, upper-crust clientele he had gotten used to. She was like a ray of sunshine breaking through the clouds, and he'd found himself thinking about her far more than any of his other students. But it was no excuse for neglecting Rachel.

"How was your day?" he asked.

With her arms still tight around him and her cheek pressed against his chest, her words were slightly muffled. But he didn't need to hear every word to know what she said. It was nearly the same every time he asked.

"It was fine. I worked on my sampler. And I read my book. And I played with Mr. Mittens."

At the sound of his name, the cat looked up from his place near the hearth and yawned. A few feet from the white-footed feline lay the discarded needlework. She'd been working on it for the past year, and had completed a section not more than a few inches across. He suspected that if he looked at the book on the shelf, he'd find her place marker hadn't moved from where it had been yesterday. He hated the idea of Rachel spending her entire day cooped up in the house doing little more than staring at the walls and talking to a cat. But there was little he could do about it.

He gave her another tight squeeze before letting her go. "Go find your hairbrush and I'll take a go at these knots before making dinner."

Her eyes narrowed into suspicious slits. "Do you promise to be gentle?"

"Of course."

"All right." She grinned and wheeled away to get the brush from her room.

She was so happy to get any attention from him. It was a pity that, no matter how hard he tried, he would pull her hair, which would make her complain, probably to the point that she would end up in tears.

Albert sighed. When had his life become so predictable? He could practically see the night unfold, like a play that he'd performed over and over again. Still, there was the possibility of a plot twist in his future.

"Albert." Rachel stood in the doorway, the tortoiseshell hairbrush clutched in her hand, her head tilted to the side. "Are you all right?"

He forced on a smile. "I'm fine. Just a touch melancholy."

She looked down at the floor, and when she looked back up there was an understanding in her eyes he wasn't used to seeing. "You take such good care of me. Please don't neglect yourself. You deserve to be happy."

Did he really? He kept Rachel hidden away like some kind of secret. Half the time he felt he was living a lie. He told himself it was for her own good as well as his, but was it? Or was he just trying to make his life easier?

Rachel giggled, and he knew the moment was gone. She skipped forward and held out the brush. "One hundred strokes, please."

He pointed to the stool by the fireplace. She settled herself down and he placed his hand gently on top of her head. "Try not to squirm, *liebling*."

As he brushed, his mind went back to Gwen, to her warm smile, her quick mind, her determination to do well on the archery range. Standing in his living room, working on the tangles in Rachel's hair, he made a decision. He may not deserve happiness, but he was going to do his best to grab a bit of it, even if he was sure it couldn't last.

Charles Drexler had to be the most boring man Gwen had ever met. He'd been at the house for three days, and every day she prayed that God would bless him with a personality. So far, her prayers had gone unanswered.

Even though she'd planned to talk to him about her father's intentions and her complete disinterest in them, she'd decided to hold off. In the spirit of "honor thy father and mother," she would take the time to get to know Charles before she told him that there would never, ever be anything romantic between them. But it was already obvious that Charles didn't care about romance any more than he cared about compatibility. He was looking for a union, yes. But his idea of marriage seemed to be one that would increase his social and financial standing in the community. The fact that he and Gwen had nothing in common didn't concern him.

That morning, when she'd left for the clubhouse, he'd again expressed his dismay that she was interested in a sport as pedestrian as archery. She could only imagine his shock and horror when he found out about her nature studies. Laughter bubbled up inside her as she imagined his face contorting in distaste at the sight of her digging in the dirt to examine a fascinating beetle or some other insect.

No, Charles Drexler was most definitely not a good match.

Gwen pushed all that from her mind as she strolled home through the forested section of Tuxedo Park. There was the usual array of flora and fauna. A pair of partridges foraged beneath a tree. Rustling amongst the foliage and a flash of brown indicated the presence of a shy dear. On any other day, she would have been on the hunt for something new to add to her field journal. But today, merely being part of nature was enough. It gave her time to concentrate on arrows and Albert Taylor.

Today, all her arrows had hit the target. None of them had hit exactly where she'd intended, but at least they'd struck a ring. It was amazing that she, Gwendolyn Banks, was learning a sport alongside other members of the community, and wasn't making a fool out of herself. Quite the contrary, if her instructor was to be believed. Albert told her she was coming along quite well, and he expected her to hit her first bull's-eye on her next lesson.

Wouldn't that be grand? He'd be so proud of her. And maybe...

Gwen's thoughts came up short as she noticed a fluttering out of the corner of her eye. It wasn't natural, like the flapping of a bird's wing, but stiff...

Gwen laughed out loud when she spotted the piece of paper secured to a tree—the same tree where she and Albert had first met—with an arrow. She held the bottom edge of the paper down so she could read the note written on it.

To Whom It May Concern,
I plan to be in this wood, in this very spot, each morning to practice my aim (although I absolutely will not aim at any butterflies nor their forest compatriots). It would please me greatly if a certain expert in the local wildlife might also

be here and share her considerable knowledge with me.

Most sincerely,

The Archer of Tuxedo Park

A thrill zinged through Gwen's heart, as if it had been pierced by an arrow straight from Cupid's quiver. She'd never received as much as a thank-you note from a man, and now here was a mysterious note from a "secret" admirer. Not that it was a great mystery who had left it, but if anyone but her had found the note, they would never have guessed the identities of those mentioned. He must have put the note there before her lesson, anticipating that she'd walk through the woods on her way home.

The idea of sharing a secret with Albert was almost as exhilarating as the idea of hitting her first bull's-eye. Not only that, but he wanted her to teach him about the creatures and plants she loved to study. No jokes, no amazement at why a woman would be interested in such a thing. But simple, honest curiosity about what interested her.

Now all she needed to do was figure out how to leave the house in the morning without Charles playing her shadow. As she neared home, Gwen began to formulate a plan. All she needed was a little luck, and the help of her sister.

The next morning, when Gwen and Matilda came down for breakfast, Matilda was done up in a lovely white day dress with layers of lace, an heirloom choker of pearls circling her neck. Matilda had told Gwen she was more than happy to assist in misdirecting Charles.

Looking at her now, Gwen knew that any man would be crazy not to want her on his arm. Gwen, on the other hand, was wearing a plain cotton frock, slightly faded from its original dark blue after many washings, but perfect for a morning of nature observations.

Charles and their parents were already seated when the sisters entered the room. Charles stood as they approached.

"Good morning, Gwen. Miss Matilda."

"Good morning, Charles," Matilda answered.

Gwen simply nodded, then moved to the sideboard to fill her plate. "I hope the food hasn't grown cold while you were waiting for us."

"Heavens no." Mother waved her hand carelessly. "Cook only just set it out."

Father cleared his throat. "Yes, but let's say grace so we can eat before it does."

Matilda reached the table first, standing behind the chair to Charles's right. He pulled it out for her to sit, and as he did so, Gwen quickly seated herself in the chair to his left. She answered Father's frown with a sweet smile, then bowed her head and clasped her hands, as did the others.

Father began to pray. "Bless us, O Lord, and these Thy gifts, which we are about to receive, from Thy bounty. Through Christ, our Lord. Amen." The rest of the table joined in on the final word together.

Mother picked up a silver toast rack and took a piece. "What do you young people have planned for today?"

Gwen pointed to her bodice. "As you can probably tell from my attire, I'm taking a nature walk this morning."

Mother set the rack down in front of Charles, but

instead of reaching for it, he looked at Gwen with confusion.

"What, pray tell, is a nature walk?"

After much talk with Matilda the night before, Gwen had decided the best idea was to be as truthful as possible. She smiled warmly as she took a piece of buttered toast and smeared it with strawberry jam. "Well, I walk through nature and make observations. When I come across something new, I note it in my field journal."

"Your field journal."

Gwen had to bite down on the inside of her lower lip to keep from laughing. The poor man was having a hard time keeping up. "Yes. It's a leather-bound book in which I make notations of what I find. I also draw sketches."

"You should see them." Matilda piped up. "Gwen really is quite a talented artist. She puts that Audubon fellow to shame."

An honest rush of embarrassment forced Gwen to look down at her plate. "That's sweet of you to say, Tilda. But Mr. Audubon is a genius. I can only aspire to be a fraction as good as he."

"You're far too modest, dear." Mother shook her head as she cut into a plump sausage link. "I've seen your work, and Matilda is right."

For a moment, Gwen was stunned into speechlessness. She'd talked to her mother on occasion about her field studies, but Gwen had never believed she was paying attention. To know that her mother actually admired what she did was a revelation.

Apparently, it was a revelation that did nothing to impress the men at the table.

"Gwen's always enjoyed doodling in those books

of hers." Father gulped his coffee, then went to work cutting the ham steak on his plate. "But I expect it's a passing fancy."

Charles nodded. "I should hope so, sir."

Gwen turned her head slowly in his direction. "Excuse me?"

Charles had the good grace to look slightly embarrassed. "I just meant to say you'll have more important things to spend your time on when you have a house of your own to care for. Especially when the children come."

"The children?" The humble warmth in Gwen's cheeks became an indignant fire. "That is an awfully presumptuous statement to make, Mr. Drexler."

"Calm down, Gwendolyn." Father leaned over and patted her hand in a dismissive manner. "Of course you're going to marry and have children. All women do. Charles didn't mean to imply anything else, did you, son?"

"No, sir." Charles snatched up his water goblet, sending some of it sloshing over the side. The faux pas only added to his discomfort, and he mumbled something that Gwen couldn't make out.

Gwen almost felt sorry for the man. Not quite, but almost. She leaned forward just enough to look past Charles and over at her sister. Matilda caught her eye and nodded slightly.

"Charles, I was wondering if you might like to accompany me into town today." Matilda laid her hand so gently on Charles's arm that she barely wrinkled the fabric of his summer suit.

Father looked at Matilda with a raised eyebrow. "What business do you have in town, little one?"

"For days I've been thinking of the sundaes at Wren's Ice Cream Parlor, and today I woke up knowing that I simply cannot wait any longer." Matilda smiled in a way that couldn't help but melt her father's heart. "May I, Father? Please?"

Mr. Banks tried to maintain his gruff look, but failed. "I suppose there's no harm, as long as your sister and Charles accompany you."

Gwen barely avoided choking on a piece of toast. Going to town with them was not part of the plan. If she couldn't get her father to agree, everything would be ruined. "Father, I have my heart set on spending my morning in the woods."

He chuckled as if amused by her foolishness. "The woods will be there tomorrow."

Charles nodded. "Besides, with your foot the way it is, you shouldn't be walking through there alone."

Gwen was about to shoot off a strong retort when she heard her father's slow, deep intake of breath. Mr. Banks might doubt his daughter's ability to land a beau on her own, but he had never coddled her when it came to her physical disability. Nor did he take kindly to people who thought Gwen less than capable because of it. Without knowing it, Charles had said the very thing that would ensure she'd be allowed to do just what she wanted.

"One thing you will learn, my boy, is that Gwen can take care of herself. She may have a limp, but she is one of the strongest people I know." This time, when Father patted her hand, she felt warmth and sincerity. "Enjoy your trek through the woods, my dear. Charles, please escort Matilda into town and enjoy the ice cream. It really is a treat."

"Thank you, Father." The sisters almost spoke in unison, bringing some much needed levity to the table.

Gwen risked a look in Charles's direction. With his pursed lips and furrowed brow, he had the appearance of someone who'd been sucking on a lemon. Let him wear his disapproval upon his face. Nothing was about to dampen Gwen's spirits.

She was now free to go on the hunt for one of Mother Nature's more elusive and rare creatures: The Archer of Tuxedo Park.

Albert was quickly doubting the wisdom of leaving his cryptic note on the tree. It was gone, so someone had found it, but who? He would be mortified if a random stranger had happened upon it and decided to walk through the woods to discover who called himself "The Archer of Tuxedo Park." But it would be even worse if Gwen had found it and chosen not to show up.

How long had he been standing out there? It seemed like hours since he'd arrived at what he was coming to think of as "their tree." Albert pulled the watch from his pocket and flicked the cover open.

He'd been waiting for all of thirty minutes.

She might have already come and, finding him not there, left. It was the one thing worse than having her not show up at all, because then she would think he was playing a joke on her. What had seemed like a clever idea yesterday was quickly beginning to feel like a recipe for disaster. "You've had some bad ideas in your day, Taylor," he muttered to himself, "but this one is right up there with the worst of them."

A laugh sounded from the trees and a moment later, Gwen stepped into view, her leather-bound journal tucked safely under her arm. "Is that a new archery strategy? Talking yourself into hitting a bull's-eye?"

He laughed, hoping to high heaven that she hadn't heard what he'd said. "Whatever works to make the shot. And how about you? Is this stealth natural or does it come from much practice?"

"Oh, it took me many, many hours of practice to develop what little stealth I have." She pointed down to her foot. "As I'm sure you've noticed, I'm clumsy by nature."

"I hadn't noticed that at all."

Gwen put a hand on her hip and looked at him askance. "Come now. You couldn't possibly have missed my limp."

"Of course I noticed the limp, but that's not the same as being clumsy."

She looked as if she was weighing her words before she spoke. "You'll have to forgive me, Albert. I'm not used to anyone speaking so openly about my physical impairment."

"We all have challenges. Some are physical, some not as apparent to the eye, but they're still there." Albert shrugged, hoping to make her feel more at ease. "I choose my friends based on their personality and character, not on whether or not they can win at a foot race."

A deep laugh burst from Gwen and she put her hand flat against her stomach. "Oh, dear, I'm certainly glad to hear that. Elsewise, you and I would have to part ways right now."

"That would be a terrible shame." He grinned, totally besotted by the charming woman in front of him. When he realized that perhaps he was looking at her a bit too intently, he searched for something else to say.

"How would I ever learn about the woodland creatures of Tuxedo Park without you as my guide?"

Her eyes sparkled with excitement. "Indeed. I should tell you, I'm not an expert by any means, but I do consider myself quite well versed in the local flora and fauna."

"How long have you been studying it?"

She thought for a moment, then opened the journal and ran her finger down the first page. "This journal dates back five years, to when father bought the cottage."

Albert withheld his opinion that anything as grand as the homes lived in by the residents of the community couldn't possibly be considered cottages. It wasn't Gwen's fault that the gentry tried to make themselves feel better about their opulence by downplaying it.

"What sparked your interest in studying nature?"

Gwen shook her head, almost as if she herself were surprised by her choice of hobby. "I know, it isn't what one expects of a lady. But the first year we vacationed here, I didn't know what to do with myself. I was working my way through all the books in the library when I came across Mary Treat's *Home Studies in Nature*. She said that, for the lover of birds, insects and plants, even the smallest area around a home could provide enough knowledge for a lifetime." She stopped, suddenly looking embarrassed, and shrugged. "Something about that made sense to me. I've been studying ever since."

"I think it's wonderful." Albert leaned his bow and his quiver of arrows against their tree. "Madam, I am your humble student. Where shall we start?"

As if on cue, the trill of a bird sounded overhead.

Gwen pointed to the branches of a tree beside him. "We can start with this beautiful fellow."

He looked up to see a flash of bright yellow as the bird hopped across the branch. "Are you sure 'fellow' is the right term? Something that pretty must be a female."

She shook her head. "Oh no. In nature, the more beautiful and brightly colored animals are almost always male. Let me show you."

Gwen began flipping through the pages of her book and Albert drew closer as if to look over her shoulder. But as the gentle breeze brushed a strand of her hair across his cheek, and he caught the scent of lemon verbena, all he could think about was that he never expected to be standing with this remarkable woman in this beautiful, peaceful setting.

Chapter 6

"Which do you think? The red or the green?"

Gwen fell back on her sister's bed, landing on a pile of discarded dresses. "What difference does it make, Tilda? Whichever one you pick will be gorgeous, and you can wear the other to the next party."

"It makes a huge difference." Matilda scowled into the full-length mirror as she held the red dress up beneath her chin. "This is the first party at the Kane house, and I want to make a good impression."

"Sister, you can't help but make a good impression."

The compliment softened Matilda's features a bit. "Thank you." She returned the red dress to the bed and picked up the green satin. "I think this is the right choice. It's lovely, but not as bold as the red. I don't want to seem impertinent."

Gwen laughed. "As if you ever could. I think that's an excellent choice."

"Very good. We've taken care of me. Now, what about you?"

"Me?" Gwen sat up quickly. "Since I plan to spend the evening in my room with a novel, I believe my choice will be a nightdress."

Matilda frowned and shook her finger at Gwen. "Oh, no. You're not going to hide away here all night. You're going to that party with me."

"Tilda, you know how I feel about parties. They're a waste of time. And they're embarrassing."

"You don't have to dance if you don't want to. And is it a waste of time spending time with your adoring baby sister?" Matilda batted her eyes coyly and pouted.

With a groan, Gwen tossed a silk-covered pillow at her. "You are shameless."

Matilda laughed. "And you're just grumpy because you're caught betwixt two men."

"Whatever do you mean? I'm not caught betwixt anybody."

"Oh, come now." Matilda laid the green dress carefully across the foot of the bed. "There is Charles, the man Father has chosen for you but in whom you have no interest. And there's Albert, the peasant archer who you can't stop thinking about, which would make Father livid if he knew."

Matilda was entirely too perceptive for her own good. Of course, it wouldn't take a great sleuth to deduce where Gwen's heart lay, especially since she'd solicited Matilda's help over the past week to distract Charles so she could spend time with Albert. No matter how hard she'd tried to tell herself that Albert was only her teacher and her friend, it was no good. She'd fallen for him, hard.

"For the life of me, I don't know why Father would think that Charles and I might be a good match."

"Oh, I can see it." Matilda began hanging up dresses to return to the closet, even though one of the maids would be in soon enough to do it. "After all, he's handsome. Charming. And he has a lovely sense of humor."

Sense of humor? "Are we talking about the same man? Charles Drexler? The sourpuss who eats his meals here and goes on and on about business and politics?"

"You just haven't spent any time getting to know the real man."

Oh no. "Tilda, when I asked for your help keeping him busy, I didn't mean for it to turn into anything else. Are you starting to have feelings for him?"

"Feelings? Don't be silly." Matilda waved away the words, although the expression on her face implied that Gwen had come closer to hitting the target than she wanted to admit. "I've simply had a chance to get to know him better than you have, that's all. He really is quite an interesting person. And quite a conversationalist."

"What do you mean?"

"He loves meeting new people. Everywhere we go, he shows such great interest in my friends. It makes them all feel quite special."

Odd. Gwen had never had cause to think that he was interested in anyone beyond himself. Maybe she really hadn't given him a fair chance. Not that she had any desire to consider him as a beau, but maybe she should consider that he might be a decent person.

Matilda came back from the closet holding a lovely beaded reticule. "At any rate, I know he'll be disappointed if you don't go tonight."

Gwen's heart dropped. "He expects to escort me tonight, doesn't he?"

"Yes, he does." Her voice dropped. "And so does Father."

Gwen sighed. They were ganging up on her. If she wanted to keep the peace and avoid an uncomfortable family scene, she would attend the party.

But she didn't have to like it.

As they walked into the Kane ballroom, it was Matilda who garnered stares of admiration. Charles wasn't able to look away from Matilda, which irritated Gwen, though she did her best to hide it. True, she didn't yearn for Charles's attention, but given that her father still saw them as a match, he could at least feign interest in Gwen.

The deep green of Matilda's dress complimented her eyes, and the intricate design of beads encrusting the bodice and sprinkled down the front of the skirt shimmered beneath the lights from the grand chandelier. Walking off to the side with her hand resting gently atop Charles's arm, Gwen felt almost invisible. Though it was exactly what she wanted, it still seemed to sting somehow.

"It's all so beautiful." Matilda sighed as she looked around the room.

Charles turned away from Gwen and looked down at Matilda. "May I get you some punch?" He then looked back at Gwen. "For both of you ladies, I mean."

Gwen barely smiled. "Yes. Thank you."

When Charles walked away, Gwen turned to her sister. "Perhaps we should talk to Father about letting Charles be your escort tonight."

Matilda looked appalled. "Gwen, no. I wouldn't do that to you."

Gwen smiled at her sister. "Do what? You're going to want to dance, and I assume Charles will want to dance. You and I both know I have no desire whatsoever to dance. It makes perfect sense."

It seemed to be an offer too good for her sister to pass up. Matilda worried her bottom lip between her teeth as she looked at the couples swirling on the dance floor. "I do love to dance."

"Then it's settled. Father!" Gwen moved to where her father was talking to a group of gentlemen and stood at his elbow, waiting for his attention.

After a moment he looked down at her and smiled. "Do you need to speak to me, Gwen?"

"Yes, please."

She drew him away a few steps and explained that she'd like to free Charles to dance with Matilda. After commending her on her sensible outlook, he gave his permission, then returned to his friends who were discussing the merits of Teddy Roosevelt.

Making her way through the crowd, Gwen found Charles and Matilda standing together, she sipping a glass of punch as he smiled down at her. Oh, yes, there was definitely something blossoming between those two. Which gave Gwen a legitimate reason to get to know Charles better.

"Ah, there you are, Gwen." Charles handed her the other cup of punch he held.

"Thank you." She sipped slowly, enjoying the dueling flavors of sweet and tart on her tongue. She turned to Matilda and smiled, then returned her attention to Charles. "I just spoke to Father, and he's given permission for you to become Matilda's escort for the evening."

"If you'd like to, of course." Matilda spoke up.

"Certainly." The lift of his brows said he didn't know how she could think he wouldn't be pleased. He glanced quickly at the dancers and looked back at Gwen. "I understand. And thank you."

It may have been the nicest thing he'd said to her in the short time that she'd known him. Matilda finished her punch, then set the glass on the empty tray of a server passing by. Her expectant look made Gwen laugh.

"I do believe my sister is ready to dance."

Charles offered his arm. "It would be my pleasure."

As the two walked together to the dance floor, Gwen felt a twinge of envy. Matilda was so elegant, she and Charles made a striking couple. And as they began the waltz, her movements were effortless. Gwen had long known she could never match her sister's graceful movements, and she'd made peace with it, for the most part. But sometimes, she couldn't help but wish things were different.

What would it be like to attend a grand party on the arm of a gentleman who truly wanted to be with her? An image of Albert Taylor sprung to mind, looking dashing in one of the new-style dinner jackets all the men were sporting. What would it be like to dance with him, to feel one hand on her waist as he cradled her fingers gently in his other?

"Good evening, Miss Banks."

Good heavens, now she was even hearing his voice. She turned to see if in fact anyone had actually spoken and nearly dropped her punch glass.

"Albert."

He reached out to steady her hand. "I didn't mean to startle you. But I suppose I'm the last person you expected to see here."

"Truthfully, yes." Villagers never socialized with the parkies. Gwen thought it a ridiculous class separation, but it was the way things were. Yet here he was, not holding a silver tray and serving as a butler, but dressed just as she'd imagined him, looking more handsome than any other man in the room.

Before she could say any more, the host of the party, Grenville Kane, came up and slapped Albert on the back. "There you are, son. If I can pull you away from Miss Banks, there are some people I want you to meet."

The imposing man moved quickly away, obviously not concerned with whether or not Gwen wanted to end their conversation. Albert looked at her apologetically as he backed away.

"I'll explain everything just as soon as I can. I promise."

Then he turned and moved with long, sure steps to catch up with Mr. Kane, who was already talking to a group of men and gesturing behind him. Gwen watched as Albert joined the group and, following quick introductions, exchanged handshakes all around.

It was indeed curious.

"Gwenie, what's going on?" Matilda bounded up to her. "Are my eyes playing tricks on me, or did I see your archery instructor friend?"

Gwen frowned. "Why aren't you dancing? Where's Charles?"

"I handed him off to my friend Sadie."

A quick scan of the dance floor and Gwen spotted

Charles dancing with a woman several inches taller than he. Oh yes, Sadie. Her height combined with her long, thin face gave her an unfortunately equine look.

Matilda shook her head. "The poor dear always comes to these things alone and rarely has the opportunity to dance. When I asked Charles, I expected him to say no, but he was happy to comply."

Another surprise. Gwen was beginning to feel like Alice falling down the rabbit hole. "That's very nice of him." Then she looked back at Albert.

"Yes, it is. But enough of that." She followed Gwen's gaze, then made an affirmative sound. "I was right. That is Albert. No wonder you wanted to free yourself of Charles."

"What?" Gwen turned her attention back to Matilda. "No, that wasn't the reason at all. I didn't even know Albert would be here."

"Why is he here?"

"I have no idea." She motioned to the crowd of men. "I think he was about to tell me, but then Mr. Kane came and pulled him over to talk to his friends."

Matilda's eyes widened. "So it's a mystery we have here. Leave it to me, sister. I'll get to the bottom of it."

Before Gwen could stop her, Matilda was off, moving to a group of women who were already clucking about some juicy piece of gossip. Surely it wouldn't take her long to turn the conversation to Albert Taylor and find out exactly what the man was doing here.

It took even less time than she expected. By the time she'd moved to a cozy seating area of chairs and couches in the corner, the orchestra had begun playing a new song and Matilda was hurrying to her side.

"That was quick," Gwen said.

Matilda settled on the couch and gave her sister a wink. "It's not my first time. There's a fabulous story behind Mr. Taylor's appearance here."

When Matilda didn't immediately share, Gwen poked her in the ribs. "Do tell."

Matilda giggled as she inched sideways. "All right. It seems that Mr. Kane has a bee in his bonnet about the Summer Games. Since they'll be held in Saint Louis, he's determined the Tuxedo Park Club be represented."

Things were beginning to make sense. "I see. So he's interested in Albert's skill as an archer."

"That's right. He's putting together a team with Albert at the head, and he's making sure all his cronies know about it."

Of course, taking a team to the world's premier athletic event would require support from the community, as well as a financial commitment. What better way to ensure both of those than to bring Albert right into the middle of Tuxedo Park society?

Matilda leaned close to Gwen and whispered in her ear. "This could be the answer to your conundrum."

"What conundrum is that?"

"Your attraction to Mr. Taylor, despite your difference in status." Matilda leaned back and smiled. "Father is much less likely to disapprove now that Grenville Kane is the man's sponsor."

Gwen was ready to counter with the fact that it didn't matter what Father thought of Albert, but then she stopped. Matilda was right. Gwen had real feelings for Albert Taylor, and this new development would make it easier for them to build a relationship. But of course there was one very important piece of information missing.

"I don't even know if he shares my feelings," Gwen said. "Most likely, he simply sees me as a friend and a student, in which case, this point is moot."

"There's one way to find out."

Matilda jumped to her feet, but Gwen snatched her wrist before she could get away. "Oh no you don't. Please, Tilda. Let's just wait and see how events unfold."

The softening of Matilda's mouth and the glow in her eyes showed she understood. "Of course. Now, if you'll release your grip, I believe I'll see if I can coax another dance out of Charles."

Gwen smiled as she watched her sister move away. The girl was full of such natural joy, she almost skipped across the room. Matilda could find the good in just about anyone, even someone as difficult to read as Charles. Gwen, on the other hand, was used to seeing the less positive side of people. She'd overheard too many unkind comments made by people who apparently thought that having a lame foot also meant she had a hearing problem.

Albert was an altogether different sort of man. He spoke with her honestly about her disability, but never belittled her because of it. He never considered her less than capable simply because of her limp.

She looked around the room and her eyes finally came to rest on Albert. Mr. Kane was still with him, but they were now talking to Mr. Kane's wife and his daughter, Eloise. Mr. Kane had apparently just made the introductions, because Eloise held up her hand. Albert took her fingers very gently and bent over them, not enough to actually kiss them, but close. When he straightened up, Mr. Kane gestured to the dancing couples. Albert smiled and said something to Eloise. She nodded. Then he took her hand and walked her onto the dance floor.

Seeing the two together made the breath catch in Gwen's throat. Eloise was a beautiful young woman: tall, but not too tall, with classic features and chestnut hair that glowed with red highlights as she moved gracefully across the floor. If Albert was positioning himself to move up in society, as a bid for the competition certainly implied, then Eloise was exactly the type of woman he should have at his side.

Gwen rose from the couch, suddenly feeling weighted. She would find her father and tell him that she planned to sit in the rear garden until the family was ready to return home. Time outside in the night air surrounded by the smells and sounds of nature would lift her spirits, and no doubt cool the heat that had blossomed in her cheeks.

Chapter 7

Albert checked his watch one more time, then slipped it back in his trouser pocket. She was ten minutes late. He'd come to expect Gwen to show up early for their walks in the woods, or right on the dot, but never had she arrived late. Perhaps she'd had a difficult time getting away from her family today. Or perhaps, she was upset about the party.

He should have told her ahead of time that they might run into each other, but he hadn't even known he'd be attending until the last minute. Mr. Kane had been hinting at it for weeks, but yesterday he'd arrived at the archery range just as Albert finished up his last lesson of the day. Mr. Kane said he would have everything Albert needed brought to his home before the party started. Thankfully, Albert had enough time to make it home before the delivery driver arrived and discovered Rachel.

But there hadn't been time to speak to Gwen, not even at the party. Mr. Kane had kept him busy interacting with everyone from the youngest socialites to the oldest doyennes of the community. There hadn't been a free moment until the orchestra began to pack up their instruments, and by that time, the Banks family had left.

The crunch of leaves behind him signaled a change. He turned and broke out into a grin. "Gwen. It's good to see you."

"I'm sorry to be late." Her voice was low and even tempered, a difference from her usual morning exuberance.

"I was afraid you decided not to come."

She hesitated. "I almost didn't."

"I'm so sorry about the party last night." He took a step closer, but her crossed arms and serious expression warned him against touching her. "I'm sure you wonder why I was there."

"I know some of the why." Gwen gazed at him with an intensity he hadn't seen before. "Matilda found out about Mr. Kane wanting to sponsor you in the games. That's wonderful news."

"Yes, it is. And you're probably wondering why I never mentioned it to you."

Gwen waved her hand as if she cared no more about it than she did about Jason Adler's automobile. "You certainly don't owe me an explanation. Although I would have been interested to know you were hoping to compete, it's your own business."

Albert sighed. "If it was only my business, I would have told you. But Mr. Kane swore me to secrecy until it was time for him to trot me out and meet his friends. Last night just happened to be my debut."

Gwen frowned. "You make it sound like you're a show pony."

"I rather felt like one last night. Soliciting is not something I enjoy doing, but it's necessary if I want to make something out of myself."

"I understand." She uncrossed her arms, but still held her journal in front of her. "It looked like you enjoyed some of the party last night. You spent a lot of time dancing."

When he saw her at the party, he knew she'd most likely seen him dancing. He'd wanted to tell her right then why he was there, but his promise to Mr. Kane prevented that. He'd thought all night about what to say when he next saw her, and he could settle on only one answer: the truth. "There are many charming ladies in Tuxedo Park. But there was only one woman I really wanted to dance with, and sadly, she was not available."

Gwen drew in a slow breath. "That's a shame. Hopefully, your lady will be available next time."

"I certainly hope so." He reached out and took one of her hands, pulling it away from her book. "In case you haven't realized, I'm talking about you."

Her eyes widened. "Me?"

"Yes, you." Albert laughed. "I know it's unusual for someone like me to express a personal interest in someone like you. But you're quite an unusual woman."

Gwen bit her bottom lip and looked down at her feet.

"Oh, no." Albert put a finger beneath her chin and tilted her head up. "I meant because of class distinctions, nothing more. And you are unusual, but in the most wonderful way."

Her eyes glistened and a careful smile pulled at the corners of her mouth. "I find you quite…unusual…as well."

"Then perhaps you'll honor me with a dance one day."

A look of terror came over her face. "I don't dance."

"Have you tried?"

"No." She gave a hard shake of her head.

"Then how do you know?"

"I just know." She pulled her hand from his and turned away. "I've never tried to fly, either, but I know I can't do that."

How hard should he push her? Certainly not enough to make her cry, but he didn't want her to think he was giving up on her, either.

"We don't have to talk about it now." He took a step away. "But I *will* ask you to dance again."

She looked over her shoulder. "You'll be at more parties?"

"Oh, yes, Mr. Kane believes I need to be visible, so I'll be as common a sight at these soirees as goose liver pâté."

Gwen laughed as she turned back around. "I'll be much happier to see you than the goose liver."

"That's good to know."

"But I'm still not going to dance with you."

Albert detected a note of challenge in her voice that he couldn't resist. "Then I hope you won't mind if I keep asking you."

She smiled shyly. "Not if you won't mind that I keep turning you down."

So that was how it would be—a battle of wills to see which one would give in first. Miss Gwendolyn

Banks was about to find out just how stubborn and determined he could be.

He let a smile slowly lift the corner of his mouth. "Agreed."

Gwen woke to sunlight streaming through her window, and a chickadee singing its distinctive song on the tree limb outside her bedroom. She stretched her arms far above her head, then wiped the sleep from her eyes with the back of one hand. Now that the whirl of gaiety had begun and parties were an almost nightly occurrence, Gwen had accompanied her family to all of them for the past week. Never before had she participated in so much. It was exhausting, but exhilarating. For once, Gwen was beginning to understand what Matilda meant when she said she wished summer would never end.

It had taken a while for Gwen to fully comprehend the depth of Albert's admission on the archery field. When the truth had finally become clear, she was in shock. Albert had feelings for her. He was genuinely interested in her, not only as a student, nor as a means to an end, but as a person. For the first time in her life, Gwen had feelings of affection for a man, and the most incredible part was that he returned them.

Albert had been as good as his word. She'd seen him at almost all the parties, and every time, he politely asked her to dance. And every time, she politely turned him down. At first, she treated it like a game, considering herself the winner when he walked away to dance with someone else. But last night, that had changed.

He had asked in the same polite way, and accepted her refusal gracefully, as he always did. But when he walked away, Gwen had not felt at all like a winner. She'd felt great disappointment. And as she watched Albert dancing with another young woman, Gwen finally realized she was missing out on something.

No more. Gwen threw back the covers and reached for her robe at the foot of the bed. Today was the day she would do something about it.

She walked carefully down the hall and tapped on her sister's door. "Matilda." Gwen rasped a greeting, then pushed the door open.

There was a lump under the covers of her sister's bed, and it sounded like the lump was crying. Gwen sat down beside her, careful not to crush an arm or leg. "Tilda, what's wrong?"

A gasp sounded, and then Matilda popped up, throwing the covers away. "Gwenie, what are you doing here?"

"I came to ask you something, but that's not important now. What's wrong?"

Matilda hung her head, shoulders slumped. "You'll think I'm being silly."

"No, I won't."

"Yes, you will."

Gwen sighed. "Perhaps I might think you're silly. But that doesn't mean I won't listen seriously to what's bothering you."

"All right." Matilda took a deep breath and sat up straighter. "It's about Charles."

"Charles?" Gwen clenched her fists. "Has he acted with you in an untoward manner?"

"Oh no, of course not. It's just the opposite."

Gwen blinked in confusion. "Excuse me?"

"He's been a perfect gentleman. Even though you

have no interest in him, and I've all but thrown myself at his feet, he treats me almost like a sister."

"I think you're exaggerating." In fact, Gwen had noticed Charles looking at Matilda several times in a most nonbrotherly way.

Matilda looked away and blew out a breath. When she looked back at Gwen, her face was serious. "I think he's still carrying a torch for you."

Gwen couldn't stop herself. She burst out laughing.

Matilda's brows pulled down into a deep frown. "It's not funny."

"Oh, yes, it really is." Gwen dabbed at the moisture gathering in the corners of her eyes. "I'm not laughing at you, Tilda, really. But the idea that Charles has ever carried anything for me other than disapproval is patently absurd."

"Then why does he talk about you all the time?"

"He talks about me?" Gwen found that hard to believe. "What does he say?"

"He talks about how Father had such high hopes for the two of you, and how he wishes the match could be possible."

Now it made sense. "I see. So he's really talking about Father, and how he doesn't want to disappoint him."

Matilda frowned. "Well, maybe. When you put it like that, I guess it could be true."

Gwen reached out and took Matilda's hand. "Trust me, sister, Charles has no interest in me. What concerns me now is the interest you're showing in him."

Truth be told, Gwen didn't believe Charles was a good match for Matilda, either. Her sister was so full of life, so vivacious. Charles was so…staid. Gwen didn't see what the appeal was. Unless it was that Matilda was so used to men fawning over her that she didn't know what to do when one didn't.

Matilda wiped the tears from her face with the corner of her bedsheet. "I don't know why you're concerned. I've spent time with Charles, mostly at your request, and I've gotten to know him quite well."

Yes, if it hadn't been for Gwen, Matilda wouldn't be in this spot right now. It was a sore point, and one that Gwen intended to remedy. Before she could reassure her sister, Matilda grabbed her wrist.

"Please, can we change the subject and speak of happy things? What brought you to my room this morning?" She leaned forward, eyes wide. "Is there news about Albert?"

The shock of finding Matilda in tears had chased the original purpose from her mind, but now it came back with a vengeance. "In a manner of speaking, yes. I have another favor to ask, but I'm fairly certain you'll enjoy this one."

"Do tell."

Gwen drew in a deep breath and collected her courage. "I want you to teach me to dance."

A radiant smile blooming, Matilda sat up on her knees and clapped her hands. "Gwenie, you have no idea how long I've waited for you to say that." Then she jumped up from the bed and held out her arms. "Let us begin."

It had been a long time since Albert had needed to bunk down in anything other than his own bed, but today, the clean straw in the empty stall was as welcoming as a down-stuffed mattress. He just needed a few minutes of rest. Just some time to close his eyes.

His lids had drifted shut before he'd finished propping himself up in the corner. The past few weeks had been draining, both physically and emotionally. He wasn't used to the unending flurry of parties. By now, he expected he would have met every resident of Tuxedo Park, but apparently he hadn't. Because every time Grenville Kane chose to trot him out, he met someone new, or at the very least, someone whom he'd barely spoken to previously and wanted to find out more about the games and what chance the Tuxedo Park Archery team had of winning a medal. It was exhausting to keep a smile on his face while answering the same questions over and over again. He was coming to thoroughly dislike the very word *party*.

The one bright spot was seeing Gwen, though their battle of wills was beginning to wear on him. He knew she was determined to stay off the dance floor, but he truly thought he'd have gotten through to her by now. Still, every time he made the invitation, she turned him down. He did his best to do as she asked and not take it personally, but each refusal delivered a bit of sting.

And then there was Rachel. She did best with a set routine, but that had been dashed over the past few weeks. Most nights, he had barely enough time to come home after work and make sure she ate before he had to change and hurry back out again. He never knew exactly when he could leave each party, so by the time he returned home he usually found Rachel pacing the floor, talking to herself. It took him hours to calm her down enough that she could fall asleep.

"Albert, wake up."

Albert's eyes flew open. At some point he'd fallen

asleep, and from the slant of the shadows on the stall wall, he'd been there for some time.

Dillon Mayhew, one of the stable grooms, leaned against the frame of the open stall door, smirking. "Those society folks have been running you ragged, eh?"

"You don't know the half of it." Albert rose slowly to his feet, working the kinks out of his back and neck.

"No rest for the weary, me boyo. Another one of them's outside looking for ya."

Oh no. He'd slept right into a lesson. "Who is it?"

"Nice woman. Don't think I've seen her here before. Walks with a bit of a limp."

"Thanks for finding me." He clapped Dillon on the back as he hurried past him. "I owe you one."

Dillon laughed and called after him. "Bring me along to one of those fancy shindigs, and I'll call us even."

How he wished he could let Dillon go to all the parties in his stead. For now, it was a necessary part of the process. Getting to the Summer Games required hard work and sacrifice. He just hadn't known the extent of it.

As he careened around the side of the barn, he ran into someone coming the other way. A flash of warm brown eyes and a startled gasp was all it took for him to realize he'd almost run down Gwen. He reached out quickly and grabbed her shoulders, keeping her on her feet.

"I'm sorry, Gwen. Are you all right?"

"I'm fine."

But she didn't seem fine. They stood close enough that he could hear the labored intake of her breath. "Are you sure? You seem to be having trouble breathing."

"Oh. Well." She looked down at his chest, then sideways to where his fingers were wrapped around her upper arm. "I just had the wind knocked out of me, I suppose. Maybe if you took a step back…"

"Of course." He immediately released her and all but jumped backward. He was acting like a buffoon. Desperately, he searched for something intelligent to say. "I'm sorry to be late for our lesson."

"It's all right. Really. But when you weren't there, I was worried about you so I asked if anyone had seen you, and someone said they saw you walk this way." She pointed down to his trouser leg. "You were definitely in the barn."

Albert was aghast to discover that straw clung to one entire side of his leg. He looked like a hobo. A buffoonish hobo.

He squeezed the back of his neck and tried not to sound as sheepish as he felt. "I've had some personal issues to deal with lately."

A look of sympathy settled in Gwen's eyes. "If you're having financial difficulties, perhaps my father could help. You shouldn't be sleeping in a barn."

"What? Oh, no." He waved his hands in front of her as though trying to erase the words from a blackboard. "I didn't spend the night here. I just needed a quiet place to get away for a moment of rest."

"Of course."

Albert snorted out a short breath of frustration. She thought he was being brave and not admitting how bad things really were. "I assure you, I'm fine. I do have an…issue at home. But I *have* a home. With four walls, a roof and a pillow for my head. I even have a cat. She's the most independent creature you'd ever hope to meet.

I could disappear for a week and when I returned she would be utterly indifferent to me."

Gwen stared at him for a moment as if trying to decide whether or not to believe him. Then she nodded and clasped her hands together in front of her. "Very well. Then there's no reason for concern."

"None whatsoever."

"Good."

"Are you ready for your lesson?"

"Most certainly."

He motioned in the direction of the archery range. "Then let us away."

Gwen turned on her heel with Albert following. She was a remarkable woman, as kind as she was lovely. Albert had no doubt that if he had been in financial straits, she would have found a way to help him but thought no less of him for it. It was just one more thing that made her so lovable.

Albert's heart clenched. At some point, his respect and admiration for her had transformed into love, despite the fact that they were separated by class distinction. There were myriad reasons why she was far out of his reach. But then, he'd thought that about competing in the games, too. It had been merely a pie-in-the-sky idea until a chance mention of it to Mr. Kane had set in motion a chain of events that changed everything. It had been Albert's experience in life that God had a way of turning situations around when you least expected it. There was no reason it shouldn't hold true when it came to a relationship between him and Gwendolyn Banks.

Still, no matter how optimistic he tried to be, or how convincing he was about his lack of problems, the issue of his sister still nagged at him. There could be no relationship with Gwen until she knew about Rachel, and there would be no relationship after she knew. Because once she found out that he'd kept his sister hidden away, she would hate him. She'd hate him for lying, for the secrets he'd been keeping. And then everyone would find out. Rachel would be hurt, his reputation would be ruined, and they'd have to move. Again.

That decided it. As much as he wanted to be completely open with Gwen, there were some things he needed to keep to himself. At least for now.

Chapter 8

"Remind me again why I thought this was a good idea?"

Gwen clutched Matilda's arm as if she were on a sinking ship and her sister were a life preserver. Matilda patted her hand and leaned in close. "Because you're just as good as any one of the people here."

She didn't bother with a response, although Gwen highly doubted the veracity of Matilda's statement. The past several weeks of parties had been daunting, but they paled in comparison to the Ashfords' Grand Ball. The Ashfords' home was so massive and well-appointed that no one bothered with the pretense of calling it a cottage. This was the Ashford Mansion, and it was filled to the brim with the upper crust of Tuxedo Park society, as well as a few families who ranked so high in the New York social set that they couldn't be bothered sum-

mering in the exclusive community. There were even
several uniformed police officers circulating amongst
the guest, just as a reminder that common thieves and
pickpockets didn't stand a chance.

It was in this setting, amongst the who's who of the
upper echelon, beneath chandeliers covered in gold leaf
and dripping with cut crystal, that Gwen had decided
to make her first foray onto the dance floor. The idea
terrified her.

"I can't do this."

"Yes, you can." Matilda pulled her farther into the
room, waving and smiling to people as they went. "Mrs.
Reynolds, so good to see you."

Gwen put on a plastic smile for those they passed,
but she couldn't keep the terror from her voice as she
whispered to Matilda. "No. I can't. Not in front of all
these people."

"Lisbeth, you look gorgeous, dear," Matilda said to
a woman nearby. She lowered her voice as she spoke to
Gwen. "And you look gorgeous, as well."

Gwen had to confess, she felt beautiful after all the
primping and preparation that had gone into preparing
for the ball. It had taken the combined effort of four
maids as well as Matilda overseeing what she should
wear and how her hair should be arranged, but when
they were done, the result was surprising. Looking in
the mirror, Gwen had barely recognized herself.

But then she'd walked out of the room and stumbled
over the truth. No matter what she did, no matter how
artfully her hair was styled, no matter how beautiful
the gown she wore, there was no way to disguise the
dragging of her foot and the limp that came with it.

Matilda had moved them to a spot near the back

wall where they could observe without being on display themselves. After a quick look around, Gwen sighed in relief.

"I don't see Albert. Maybe he won't be at this party."

"Let's hope you're wrong, Gwenie. I'd hate to think all our lessons were going to waste."

Matilda had been quite a sport. Over the past two days, she'd taught Gwen a basic box step and worked with her until Gwen could approximate a passable waltz. She maintained that if Gwen kept her upper body straight and her arms in the proper position, no one would have a clue that her feet were shuffling beneath her floor length skirt.

But now Gwen was sure she'd been wrong. There were so many people, there was no doubt in her mind that everyone would notice everything. She'd be a laughingstock for thinking she could attempt something that required such grace and finesse.

"Besides, if Mr. Kane is determined to introduce Albert to well-connected men who could back him in the competition, this is the place to do it. Do you see that man over there?" Matilda managed to motion surreptitiously with her chin to a heavyset man who was nearly bald save for the bushy tufts above his ears. "That's Mr. Winchester. He owns the Winchester Archery Company."

"I've never seen him before. Does he live in the park?"

Matilda shook her head. "No, he's visiting from Pennsylvania. But he's exactly the kind of person Albert needs to meet."

Gwen gulped. Yes, there was little doubt that if Albert wasn't already here, he would arrive soon. But maybe he wouldn't ask her to dance this time. It was possible that with so many people to talk to, he wouldn't have time to dance with her, let alone ask her a question he thought he already knew the answer to.

Then, as if God had decided to play a joke on her, she saw Albert walk through the ballroom door, followed by none other than Charles. There they were, her dream and her nightmare. The man she looked forward to seeing, and the man she didn't care if she ever saw again. Unfortunately, Matilda still did care. She looked in the same direction and let out a little squeal.

"Oh, there they are. And don't they look dashing?"

Gwen nodded. Yes, indeed they did. She may not care for Charles, but he was a handsome man. As for Albert…words could not describe what she felt when she looked at him.

Matilda pulled against her, straining to get away as if she was a racehorse pulling against the bit. Gwen was still concerned about her sister's interest in Charles, but she had no concrete reason to keep her away from him.

"Go have fun." Gwen released her viselike grip on her arm.

Matilda grinned, but didn't immediately dash away. "Are you sure? Will you be all right?"

"I'll be fine. I just panicked a bit. I can take care of myself."

"Of course you can." Matilda planted a quick peck on Gwen's cheek, then hurried away.

Of course Gwen could take care of herself. She'd been doing it for a long time. But she was still more comfortable communing with nature and traipsing through the forest, or poking around in the garden behind her family's cottage, than mingling inside with other human beings. She understood plants and birds and insects and animals. People, on the other hand, continued to baffle her.

Perhaps some punch would help calm her. At the very least, it would give her something to do with her hands. She turned to look for a waiter, but found herself watching Albert make his way to her. As he drew closer, his eyes widened.

"Miss Banks, may I say that, although I find you beautiful every day, you look particularly lovely tonight." He offered her his hand, leaning slightly forward at the waist.

A blush warmed Gwen's cheeks as she put her hand in his. "Thank you, Mr. Taylor. You look dashing, as always."

He lifted her hand and brushed his lips lightly across her knuckles. "This new type of dinner jacket isn't the most comfortable thing I've worn, but I must admit, it seems to flatter each man who wears one."

Even when he released her hand, Gwen felt the heat from his fingers. Her mouth had gone completely dry. Where was a waiter with a punch tray when she needed one? "They've taken to calling them tuxedos," she stammered. "After the park. Since the men here brought them into vogue."

Albert shook his head, no doubt finding the notion as pretentious as she did. Gwen didn't know what to say now. Usually, they talked about archery, wildlife, the games, their favorite books and any number of interesting topics. Usually, conversation between them was easy. But tonight, as the orchestra played and couples swirled, there was one topic that neither of them seemed eager to bring up.

"Albert, I—"

"Gwen, I—"

They spoke in unison, abruptly cutting each other off. He motioned for her to continue, but she shook her head. "No, you first. Please."

"All right." Albert cleared his throat. "Gwen, I fully intended to ask you to dance with me every time I saw you, from now until the end of summer, if that's what it took. But I'm beginning to feel a bit uncomfortable being so persistent. So my question tonight is, how long should I continue to ask you?"

Gwen exhaled a slow breath. He hadn't grown tired of waiting. He still wanted to dance with her. Suddenly, the other people in the room didn't matter. Somehow, the world had narrowed down to simply Gwen and Albert, and there was no doubting what she wanted.

"One more time," Gwen said. "If you would please ask me just one more time."

Albert raised his chin as if not entirely sure what this meant. But then, for the second time that evening, he held out his hand, palm up. "Would you do me the honor of a dance, dear lady?"

Her fingers slid into his. "It would be my greatest pleasure, kind sir."

His eyes lit up and a smile played across his handsome face. As they walked slowly to the dance floor, Albert giving her plenty of time to set the pace, she knew she'd made the right choice.

What he had anticipated would be a dreadful evening had turned into a remarkable night. Mr. Kane had introduced him to several other influential businessmen who actually seemed to take his bid for the competition seriously. Mr. Winchester had been particularly positive. But the highlight of the evening had been the times when he could pull himself away from the campaigning and steal time for a dance with Gwen.

Her longtime reticence had nearly convinced him that she'd never step on the floor with him, but when she did, he was surprised at how easily she moved. Her slightly sheepish admission that Matilda had helped her practice charmed him. Obviously, she didn't want to make a fool of herself, but she had also wanted to make him proud. It was a heady and humbling realization.

Someone bumped into Albert, almost knocking him into a small table covered with discarded plates. "Excuse me, Taylor."

He was surprised to see that it was Charles. "Is something wrong?"

"I'm afraid so." He looked quickly over his shoulder. "It's Gwen. She was on her way to the garden when she tripped and fell. You know how clumsy she is."

Albert clenched his jaw to hold back a sharp retort about Charles's own clumsiness. Gwen was no more clumsy than anyone else he knew, less so when considering what she had to contend with. Still, this man wasn't worth the energy it would take to correct him. "Where is she?"

"Matilda and I helped her into one of the sitting rooms so she could prop her leg up on a settee." He straightened his tie and smoothed down the lapels of his coat. "I told her to relax, but she's asking for you."

"Of course. Which room is it?"

"Down the main hall, all the way down to another hallway on your left. Then down that hall to the last door on your right. Can you remember that?"

Did the man think him incompetent? "Yes, I can."

"Good." Without another word, Charles hurried away in the opposite direction from the one he'd just indicated.

Albert fumed. The man had no class, no consideration for others. As Albert stalked out of the ballroom, he passed Matilda on her way in.

"Is Gwen all right?" he asked.

Her brows rose in concern. "What do you mean? I haven't seen her in hours. I thought she was with you."

"You and Charles didn't just help her to a room?"

Matilda shook her head. "No. What are you talking about?"

There wasn't time to explain. "Please excuse me, Matilda." After a curt nod, Albert hurried away.

Something didn't feel right. Why would Drexler tell him Matilda had helped get Gwen settled, yet Matilda had no idea what he was talking about? And why had they put her all the way on the other side of the house? Surely they could have found a closer sitting room.

He rounded the corner and jogged to the end of the hall, then pushed his way through the door without bothering to knock. He was shocked to find himself not in a sitting room, but in a bedroom. From the looks of it, someone had been going through the bureau drawers. Several of them were half-open and clothing was strewn about the floor.

A moan drew his attention, and he looked down. A lump in dark blue satin lay between a dressing table and the massive four-poster bed.

"Gwen!"

Albert rushed to her side. As he knelt beside her, he

pulled her close and cradled her head in his lap. She moaned again and looked up at him.

"Albert? What happened?"

"I don't know. I found you here. Did you fall?"

She started to shake her head but winced and squeezed her eyes shut. "I don't think so. I think...I think someone hit me." Her eyes flew open and filled with tears as she looked up at him. "Why? Why would anyone do that?"

"I don't know. Shh, now. Just rest."

His fingers threaded through the hair at the back of her head, and his stomach roiled. He felt something warm and wet.

Blood.

Help. He needed help.

He lifted his head to call out, but a commotion in the hallway stopped him. A moment later, the open door was filled with the hulking frames of two police officers. Behind them, Albert caught a glimpse of another face. It was Charles Drexler, looking grim, yet somewhat self-satisfied.

"Don't move," one of the officers called out, drawing his firearm while the other ran forward and grabbed Albert.

"No." Gwen's voice was weak, but she fought to be heard. "Don't take him, please."

The officer hauled Albert up against Gwen's protest, leaving her once more alone on the bedroom floor.

"You've got to help her," Albert said. "She has a head wound. She's bleeding."

"We can see that." The other officer motioned with the muzzle of the gun to Albert's once-white shirtwaist. Now it was stained with blood.

Gwen's blood.

The police officers pulled him out of the room and down the hall. The closer they got to the ballroom, the more people lined the walls. Shame raked across Albert as the same people that earlier that evening had praised his ambition now glared at him with suspicion. But there was only one person he cared to speak to now.

"Matilda!"

Matilda ran up to him and stopped dead in her tracks, forcing the officers to stop, as well.

"Miss, we need to get him to the station," the first officer said.

"Not yet. I need to ask about my sister." Matilda looked up at Albert. "What happened?"

He shook his head. "I don't know. I found her on the floor. She'd hurt her head."

The other officer pulled on his arm. "That's enough. Save the confession for later."

"I'm not confessing," Albert growled. "I didn't do anything wrong."

"Sure, buddy. No one ever does."

Albert turned back to Matilda. "I didn't hurt her. I swear, I would never hurt her."

"I know you wouldn't. She trusts you, and so do I."

In the past, he'd considered Matilda somewhat superficial, but he saw a strength in her eyes now, one that enabled him to trust her with the only other thing as important as Gwen's welfare. There was no way for him to know how long the police would keep him. This was the only chance he had. "Please, someone needs to look after my cat."

"Your cat?" She was understandably confused.

"Yes." Albert stared her straight in the eye, trying

to translate the importance. "My cat. Rachel. Someone needs to go to my house and take care of her. She won't know what to do without me. Gwen will understand."

He hoped she would. He hoped she would understand all of it.

To the best of her recollection, Gwen's head had never hurt so much as it did the next morning. Waking in her own bed with the sun shining and the birds singing, she forgot for a moment that her world had been turned upside down the night before.

Then she remembered the look on Albert's face when the police had dragged him away.

She sat up, threw off the covers and immediately regretted the speed of her actions. The room tilted and spun while she gripped the edge of the mattress with both hands and prayed not to get sick all over herself.

"Thank the good Lord you're awake." Mother rose from the chair beside her bed and moved to Gwen's side. "But you shouldn't be trying to get up. You went through quite an ordeal last night."

After gently pushing Gwen back down against the pillow, Mother went to the bedroom door and looked out into the hall. One of the maids must have been waiting right outside, because Gwen heard Mother issuing directions.

"Please tell Mr. Banks that Gwen is awake. And bring up some tea and broth. Thank you, Mary."

Gwen didn't want to eat or drink anything. She wanted to know what had happened to Albert. But the set of her mother's mouth when she turned around convinced Gwen to stay quiet for the moment.

"You gave us quite a fright, young lady." Mother settled on the edge of the bed and brushed a lock of hair from Gwen's forehead.

Heavy footsteps on the stairs announced her father's arrival moments before he blustered through the open doorway. His eyes met hers and a sigh of relief rushed past his lips. "Seeing those lovely eyes of yours is an answer to prayer."

Gwen wasn't used to such openly affectionate comments coming from her father. She blinked twice, holding back the tears that brought tingles to her nose. "I'm sorry, Father. I didn't mean to worry you."

Father wagged a scolding finger at her. "Don't go apologizing for something that isn't your fault. Unless you asked that villager to knock you senseless, you aren't responsible for what happened."

"Albert didn't hurt me." Moving more slowly this time, she scooted up in the bed until her back was pressed against the headboard.

"Now, dear, you mustn't agitate yourself." Mother patted her hand. "The doctor said your recollections might be a bit muddied today. A police officer told us exactly what happened."

Frustration bubbled up inside Gwen. Yes, her head hurt beyond anything she'd thought possible, but that didn't mean she couldn't think clearly. "How would he know what happened? There was nobody with me."

Father crossed his arms over his chest. "He said a witness saw Mr. Taylor drag you down the hall and into that room. He was concerned that something nefarious was going on, so he fetched two officers."

Mother shuddered. "Thank goodness that person was there. I can't bear to think what might have happened to you."

"No, that's all wrong." Gwen pressed her fingers against the bandage that circled her head. If only the pain would stop for a second, then she could explain things as she knew them and make them understand. "Albert did not drag me into that room. I was looking for a way to the garden, and I got lost. When I opened the door to the room, I saw someone rifling through one of the bureaus."

"Do you know who it was?" Mother asked.

"No. I could tell it was a man—he was wearing a tuxedo—but his face and hair were covered."

Father nodded. "That proves it. Taylor was wearing a tuxedo. You walked in on him committing robbery, and he attacked you."

"No." Gwen's firm reply seemed to surprise her father. "It wasn't Albert. I know that with absolute certainty."

"Then you're saying one of the residents of the park did this to you? One of our friends?" Father asked. "That's absurd."

"It's true." Why would anyone be so adamant that Albert had done this, when she knew very well he hadn't? She was positive Albert had not dragged her into any room, so how could this witness have seen that happen? "Where is Albert?"

Father's mouth twitched beneath his mustache. "Where he belongs. In a holding cell at the police station."

"No, they can't hold him. They have no reason. I refuse to press charges."

"You don't need to," Father said. "The Ashfords have charged him with burglary."

"How can they do that? They have no proof!" As

her voice rose and she leaned forward, the room once more began to spin.

"Dear, please. Calm down." Mother stroked her shoulder.

Father looked at her with sad eyes. "I'm sorry, Gwen, but they do have proof. They found a piece of family jewelry in his jacket pocket."

No. It wasn't possible. Albert was no thief. He was the kindest, most honest man she'd ever met. He would never hurt anyone—he would never hurt *her*.

But he had been experiencing a great deal of stress in his bid for the upcoming competition. Then she remembered finding him at the clubhouse after he'd obviously been sleeping in the barn. Although he denied being destitute, she knew he had some kind of problem at home. Could those things have prompted him to follow in another archer's path? To rob from the rich and give to the poor, which in this case would be himself?

Of course, it was possible. The problem was, it wasn't remotely probable. None of it made sense.

Her head was pounding. Mother was right. She needed to rest.

"I think I'd like to lie back down for a while."

Mother nodded. "I'll have Mary hold back the tea until later."

After her parents had left the room, she pulled the covers up to her forehead and curled into a ball beneath them, as she had when she was a little girl and wanted to hide. When one of the children at school was mean to her and called her names, she would come home and burrow under her blankets, imagining she was in a secret cave and if she wished very, very hard, she'd be able to disappear. She was too old to believe such things now, but the mere act brought a small amount of comfort.

A moment later, she heard the turn of the doorknob and the click of the latch. Mother must not have been able to stop Mary from bringing up the tray.

"I'm not hungry," she called from under the covers.

A female voice answered. "That's good, because I didn't bring any food."

"Matilda?" Gwen pulled down the cover just enough to peep out over the top.

"Oh, Gwenie, I'm so glad you're all right." Matilda dropped to the bed and gathered up Gwen in a bear hug, sheets and all. "I was so scared."

"Thank you, Tilda. But if you squeeze me any tighter, I fear my head might pop off."

Matilda sat back abruptly. "Oh, dear. I'm sorry. I should let you rest, but I have something very important to tell you." She leaned in closer. "Do you have the strength to talk?"

Gwen wasn't sure she had the strength to do much of anything, but Matilda had her attention now. "Is it about Albert?"

"Yes." Matilda nodded.

"Then I want to hear what you have to say."

"All right." Matilda drew in a deep, steadying breath. "I saw him last night, when the police were taking him out."

"He didn't do it, you know," Gwen interrupted.

"I know. I told him as much."

A glow warmed Gwen's chest. She really could count on her sister. "Thank you. Continue."

"Well, he professed his innocence, told me that

you had been hurt, and then he said something very strange."

"What was it?"

"He asked me to look after his cat."

Surely Gwen had heard her wrong. "His cat? Are you sure?"

"Yes, quite sure. Let me see if I can remember everything he said." The tip of Matilda's tongue poked from the corner of her mouth as she looked up in the ceiling in concentration. "He said someone needed to go to his home and look after his cat because she wouldn't know what to do without him. Then he said you'd understand."

Why would he be thinking about his cat at a time like this? She could only recall him talking about the animal once before. What was it he'd said? Oh yes, that the cat was hugely independent and probably wouldn't notice if Albert went missing for a week or more. Then why was he suddenly worried about the cat's welfare?

Because it was a message. There was something at Albert's home he wanted them to find. And he probably wanted them to find it before the authorities turned his place upside down looking for evidence against him. She had to do it, but she didn't even know where he lived. And if she did, how would she get there? She was in no shape to walk. Like it or not, Gwen needed assistance.

She looked up at Matilda. "I need your help."

"Whatever you need."

Gwen held up a hand. "You might want to think about it. When Mother and Father find out, they will most certainly be mad. Are you sure you want to be part of it?"

Matilda smiled in a conspiratorial way Gwen hadn't

seen since the time they'd booby-trapped the kitchen cookie jar. "I'm beyond sure. What do you need?"

Her sister's words were exactly what Gwen had hoped to hear.

"Tilda, has Mr. Adler regained his driving privileges yet?"

Chapter 9

The holding cell of the county police department made Albert yearn to be back in the Tuxedo Park stables. At least the stall he'd fallen asleep in had been empty. And clean. And had only smelled of horses.

Had it only been three days ago that he'd been frustrated about juggling his work, raising support for the competition, figuring out how to tell Gwen about Rachel? Looking back, it all seemed so simple. Now he was facing bogus charges of burglary and assault. He'd been publically humiliated, providing grist for the rumor mill and essentially guaranteeing that no one in Tuxedo Park would want to be associated with him, let alone be represented by him in Saint Louis.

But his two biggest concerns were the women in his life. Was Gwen all right? Had Matilda given her the message, and if so, had she understood it? If she had, then the woman he was in love with would be meeting the woman he'd been hiding. Ironically, that might mean the safest place for him would be right where he was, behind bars.

The door at the front of the holding area opened, producing the now-familiar squeal of hinges desperately in need of oiling. A man in a slightly worn day suit entered, followed by a uniformed police officer. The man in the suit kept his eyes forward, blatantly ignoring the insults and slurs that were hurled from the incarcerated on either side of him. The officer, however, seemed to enjoy not only disciplining the behavior, but encouraging it. He ran his baton across the bars as he walked by, adding to the cacophony and managing to smash the occasional knuckle in the process.

Finally, the man in the suit stopped in front of the crowded cell. "Albert Taylor." He looked squarely at Albert, not hesitating to wonder which one he was.

Albert rose from the bench and approached the bars. "I'm Albert."

"I'm Detective Sutter. I've got a few questions about your case." He turned to the other man. "Officer Wyatt, we need to move him to an interrogation room."

The officer looked at Albert and nearly growled. "Step back, then."

Albert barely jumped back in time to avoid getting hit with the baton. One of the other men who had moved to the bars wasn't so lucky. He howled and backed away, holding his hand to his chest. Albert could see blood beginning to ooze through the fellow's fingers.

Detective Sutter frowned, but held his tongue. When the cell door was open, Officer Wyatt motioned to Albert.

"Out with ya, now. I don't have all day."

Albert was tempted to ask the officer how many more fingers he had to bash with his club in order to fill his daily quota. Instead, he hurried through the door, careful to keep his hands close to his body. As soon as he was clear, the officer slammed the door and locked it.

"This way." Detective Sutter took a firm grip on Albert's upper arm and led him back down the hall. Once they were out of the holding area, they turned a corner and went down a rather dismal corridor with small doors on either side.

"Number three," Officer Wyatt said from behind them.

Detective Sutter opened the door and motioned Albert in. But when the officer tried to follow, he stopped him. "That's okay, Wyatt. I've got it from here."

The officer appeared surprised. "You sure? This one's tricky."

Albert had no idea what the officer was talking about. He'd been in the prison for less than twenty-four hours and had done little more than sit inside his cell, pondering his fate. How did that translate into being tricky?

Thankfully, Detective Sutter didn't take the bait. Instead, he took a step forward, backing the officer out and slowly shutting the door as he spoke. "I'm positive. Please don't let me keep you from the important work you have to do." The door clicked shut, and before the detective turned around, he added, "Like breaking bones and drowning puppies."

Once they were alone, the detective became a bit more personable. "Please have a seat, Mr. Taylor."

There were only three objects in the room: one battered table and two uncomfortable-looking chairs. Albert sat in one, while Sutter settled in the other. The detective took a small notebook and a pencil stub from an inside jacket pocket. He flipped through the pages until he came to one covered in notes.

"Mr. Taylor, did the officers who arrested you explain your rights?"

"Yes."

"Very good. I would like to remind you that anything you say to me can and will be used against you in a court of law. Is that clear?"

Albert nodded. "Yes, it is."

"Very good. Mr. Taylor, you've been charged with burglary and assault. It's my understanding that you claim to be innocent on both counts. Is that correct?"

"Yes it is. And yes, I did say that. Because I am innocent. I know you hear that all the time, but it's true. I didn't steal anything, and I would never hurt anyone, especially Gwen."

Detective's Sutter eyebrow raised just a touch when Albert said Gwen's name. He should have called her Miss Banks, but it was difficult to adhere to etiquette when your life was on the line.

Albert leaned forward. "Detective, you have to believe me. I didn't do what I'm being accused of."

"Oh, I do believe you."

The words echoed in Albert's ears until he wasn't sure if Sutter had said them, or he'd imagined them. "You do?"

"Yes." He looked down at his notebook. "I haven't spoken to everyone who was at the party, but enough of them to catch a recurring theme. No one expected anything like this from you. They all describe you as friendly, charming and sincere. Or some form thereof. Especially that Matilda Banks. She is quite a little spitfire." He smiled, making Albert think he'd had more than a passing conversation with Matilda. Then the detective hurried on. "Of course, people speaking well of your character is not enough to exonerate you. You'd be amazed how friendly, charming and sincere some killers are."

Albert winced at the comparison. "Then why do you believe me?"

"Because this wasn't the first robbery to take place during a party held in Tuxedo Park this season. There have been several others."

"Really? I hadn't heard anything about it." Albert was surprised. The society grapevine should have been buzzing with such news.

Sutter nodded. "The upper crust doesn't enjoy being the subject of anything negative. If word got out about the robberies, how long do you think it would take before people decided to keep themselves, and their valuables, at home?"

Not long at all, which would destroy the season for all of them. "I take it you've been investigating all the robberies."

"I have. So I already have the guest list for each party, as well as what was taken." Sutter tapped the notebook with the end of the pencil. "I have to tell you, Taylor, it wasn't looking good for you. I started checking the lists and it looked like you'd been at all of them. But then, I found your open window. The Baskins reported several valuable pieces of jewelry stolen from their party last week. But you aren't on the guest list."

Albert remembered that Mr. Kane had tried to convince Mr. Baskin to allow Albert to attend, but the host had been adamant. He didn't want anyone stumping at his party. Mr. Kane had been livid, but there was no getting around it. Albert had been thrilled because it meant he could spend a quiet evening at home.

"Of course, it's thin," Sutter continued. "The fact that you didn't attend a party where jewelry went missing could simply mean that another thief was at work that night. Or it could mean that Mrs. Baskin is becoming a bit forgetful. Or that Mr. Baskin saw it as an opportunity to sell off some pieces without Mrs. Baskin's knowledge."

"Or it could mean that I'm innocent," Albert insisted.

"Calm down, Taylor. Believe it or not I'm on your side. I've got my eye on someone else."

"Charles Drexler." The name popped out before Albert could consider the wisdom of keeping it to himself.

The detective didn't specifically confirm or deny. "I find it interesting that Mr. Drexler's story not only contradicts yours, but I haven't been able to find one other person to corroborate it. What do you know about the man?"

"Not much." Albert had been far more interested in Gwen, but he tried to recall what she'd told him about Charles. "I believe he works for Mr. Banks. He's been staying with the family this summer." There was something else, something that was probably important, but he wasn't sure how to reveal it without being indelicate. "I've noticed that he has a tendency to be very friendly with members of the opposite sex. He has escorted Miss Matilda to more than one dance, but he then spends most of his time dancing with other women."

The detective looked down at his notebook. "Have you noticed him spending an inordinate amount of time with April Falconer, Odette Pettibone or Victoria King?"

"Yes."

"To which one?"

"To all three. Also Sandra Shelley and Beatrice St. Claire."

"You're sure?"

"Quite," Albert said. "All of those young ladies tend to be wallflowers. For one reason or other, they don't get much attention from available gentlemen, so they hang back. That's why it made an impression on me that Drexler was so attentive to them all."

After flipping a few more pages in the notebook, Sutter found what he was looking for. "Thank you, Mr. Taylor. That information is a great help."

"Does that mean I can go?"

Detective Sutter laughed, but there was no humor in the sound. "I'm afraid not. Unfortunately, there are a few very vocal members of the community who believe that simply being a villager makes you guilty."

Albert cursed under his breath, then immediately regretted the outburst. "Forgive me. But being judged by one's station is a heavy weight."

"I understand, and I agree. The class system is pure rubbish, to my mind. If we believe each human was created in God's image, which I do, then how can we say one is better than the other based on what job he holds or what section of town he lives in?" The detective pushed away from the table and leaned back in his chair. "As far as I'm concerned, being a villager is no more an indicator of your guilt than anything else. But there's still the fact that Drexler has stepped forward as a witness. And there's the unsettling detail of the brooch that was found in your jacket pocket."

Yes, that evidence was damaging. When they'd brought him into the police station and searched his person, he'd been shocked when one of the officers had produced it. "I still have no idea how that got there. Although it's possible that Charles slipped it in my pocket when he told me where to find Gwen."

"Yes, that is possible. But we need more than possibilities. So for now, you will remain a guest of the police department until we can find something more concrete."

"I understand." Albert didn't like it, but the detective's reasoning made sense.

"You should also know that I'll be going to your home today, looking for evidence." He leaned forward and looked Albert directly in the eye, as if to challenge him. "If you're innocent, then I shouldn't find anything."

"You won't find anything."

At least not any stolen jewelry or anything else to tie him to the robberies. But would they find Rachel?

Somehow, Albert believed the discovery he was keeping a woman secreted away at his home might cause more damage than being labeled a thief.

Getting out of the house proved to be more difficult than Gwen had anticipated. Matilda had helped her get dressed, an enterprise which took close to thirty minutes thanks to the pain in Gwen's head slowing her down more than usual. Once Gwen was ready, Matilda had gone downstairs to make sure the way was clear. She came back a few moments later to report that Mother and Father had settled themselves in the sitting room opposite the stairway landing, making it impossible for the sisters to leave without being seen.

Now Gwen and Matilda sat on the bed in Gwen's room, staring at each other in morose contemplation.

"What do we do now?" Matilda asked.

"I don't know." Gwen wagged her head slowly, careful not to jar it. "If Mother and Father see us trying to leave the house, they'll stop us for sure. We need a distraction."

She considered praying for divine intervention, but it seemed unlikely God would send someone to help her deceive her parents.

A few moments later, a rumbling sounded outside. It grew steadily louder until it sounded as if it was directly under Gwen's window.

"That sounds like an automobile." Matilda was on her feet and at the window before Gwen could agree with her.

Matilda pushed the window sash all the way up and leaned out over the sill. "Oh, my."

"Who is it?" Gwen asked.

"It's the police." Matilda pulled herself back in so quickly, she thumped her head on the bottom of the window. "They must be here about Albert."

Gwen frowned. No doubt they wanted to question her about what had happened the night before. There was no way she could leave now. She had to tell the police what she knew and hope it would exonerate Albert. However, it might make it easier for one of them to slip out.

"I think I have a plan." Gwen lowered her voice to a whisper and crooked her finger for Matilda to lean closer. "It may require some exaggeration on your part."

Matilda's lips quirked into a mischievous grin. "I'm up to the task, sister."

Gwen smiled in return. She'd expected nothing less.

Within ten minutes of the policemen's arrival, Mother had knocked on Gwen's bedroom door. She was quite surprised to find Matilda perched on the edge of the bed, and Gwen sitting fully dressed in a chair by the window.

"Being in my nightclothes all day would make me feel like an invalid," Gwen said. "I asked Matilda to help me get dressed. That and sitting in the sunshine is doing wonders for my constitution."

"That's wonderful, dear." Mother glanced toward the open door before continuing. "I'm sorry to have to ask you this, but there's a detective downstairs, and he wants to speak to you. I told him you were resting and I didn't want you disturbed, but he is most insistent."

Matilda sat up a little straighter on the bed. "Is it Detective Sutter?"

"Yes, it is," Mother said. "How did you know?"

"I met him last night. He was speaking to people at the Ashfords'. I tried to tell him that he had the wrong man, but he refused to listen to me." Matilda rose with an indignant huff. "Forgive me, Mother, but I cannot abide being in the same room as that man. I believe a walk would do me some good."

As Mother watched Matilda fly from the room, Gwen held back a grin. It was fortuitous that Matilda already knew the detective. Gwen didn't know whether she truly had such strongly negative feelings for the man, but it had certainly worked for their purpose. The original plan had been for Matilda to take umbrage with something one of the police officers said, refuse to be in the same room as him, and then stalk off as a cover for finding Jason Adler and enlisting his services to carry out the rest of their plan. But this worked just as well.

"Well..." Mother's voice trailed off in the wake of Matilda's stormy exit. "I can only assume Detective Sutter learned all he needed to from your sister last night."

"And then some, no doubt." Gwen stood slowly, glad to note that her legs felt far less shaky then they had before. "Shall we go downstairs and speak with our guest?"

Mother nodded and walked Gwen out of the room and down the stairs, keeping one hand on her elbow at all times. Normally, the protective gesture would have bothered Gwen, but now it added a bit of much-needed security.

Inside the sitting room, Father stood talking to a man who had the shocked look of someone who'd been unexpectedly dressed down. It seemed Hurricane Matilda had given him a word or two before she swept by.

"Detective Sutter," Mother spoke up. "This is my eldest daughter, Gwendolyn."

He held out his hand. "Miss Banks. I'm sorry to make your acquaintance under such circumstances."

Gwen smiled wanly, hoping to elicit more of the man's sympathy. "Yes, it is all quite distressing."

"I assure you, as I have your parents, that I have no intention of making this more difficult on you. I simply have a few questions. May we sit?"

"Of course."

Gwen chose the middle of the davenport and was quickly flanked by her parents. Detective Sutter sat in a large wing-backed chair positioned at an angle, requiring him to sit sideways in order to look her in the eye.

"Miss Banks, you were found—" he looked down at his notebook "—in the bedroom of Miss Emily Ashford. How did you end up there?"

"I was looking for a way into the garden, and I became lost. I've never been to the Ashfords' before. The layout is quite complex."

"You're right about that," the detective agreed. "I got lost a few times myself, just during my investigation last night. Party invitations to that home should come with a map."

Gwen smiled, but offered no further information. She wanted to make this interview last as long as possible, despite everyone's insistence not to tire her. She had to give Matilda enough time to finish her task.

The detective continued. "I'm curious why you were looking for the garden by yourself."

"She always does that," Father interjected. "Our Gwen is an observer of nature. She's fascinated by things that would send other females into a fainting spell."

Had she detected a trace of pride in her father's voice? The notion was almost enough to distract her from the task at hand. "Yes, I make it a point to see the gardens of every house I visit."

The detective looked doubtful. "Even with all the dancing and music going on inside?"

"People find beauty in different places," Gwen said simply. "Have you ever seen a spider's web glimmering beneath the light of a full moon?"

"No, miss, I don't believe I have."

"You should. It's a breathtaking sight."

Detective Sutter cleared his throat. "I'm sure it is. So…you were looking for the garden, but you became lost and entered a bedroom. Do you remember what happened next?"

Beads of perspiration broke out on Gwen's forehead and a chill shook her. How she wished she didn't remember. Father put an arm around her shoulders and pulled her to his side.

"I opened the door and realized I'd gone the wrong way. And then I was turning to leave the room when I saw a man rifling through one of the bureaus. Before I could make a sound, he rushed at me."

Gwen stopped and tried to take a deep breath, but something seemed to be blocking the air, keeping it out of her lungs.

Detective Sutter leaned forward. "Do you need a moment, Miss Banks?"

Mother had already grabbed Gwen's hand. "I told you this would be too much for her. You'll have to go away. She can talk to you later."

"No." Gwen forced out the word. She had to do this now, or they'd continue to believe Albert had hurt her. "No, I'll be fine. I just need a moment."

Now that the air seemed to move through her again, she calmed down. A few slow breaths later, she was able to speak.

"The man pushed the door shut and reached for me, but I stepped sideways and fell. I must have hit my head on something, because everything went black."

"We found traces of blood on a small table by the bed," Detective Sutter said. "I believe you hit your head on that."

It made sense. "The next thing I remember, Mr. Taylor was running into the room to save me."

"To save you?" The detective scribbled something in his notebook. "That's how you remember it?"

"Yes, because that's the way it happened. Mr. Taylor found me and stayed by my side until your officers took him away."

Father squeezed her shoulder again. "You'll have to forgive her, Detective. The doctor said her memory might be a bit muddled for the next few days."

"My memory is just fine." Gwen gave her father a cross look, then turned to Detective Sutter. "I remember exactly what happened. The man at the bureau had on a mask of some kind, but I know it wasn't Albert Taylor. Albert came in later and found me on the floor."

Detective Sutter scratched the back of his head. "I see. We have a witness who claims to have seen Mr. Taylor drag you down the hall and take you into that room."

"Oh, dear." Mother waved her hand furiously in front of her face.

It was all Gwen could do to stay sitting down. "He did nothing of the kind. I wandered into that room by accident and of my own free will. Mr. Taylor did not lay a hand on me. Who is this witness? I demand to know who's spreading such lies."

A whisper of a smile twitched across the detective's lips, making Gwen wonder if he'd been hoping all along that she'd ask that question.

"The witness is Mr. Charles Drexler."

"Charles?" All three of them said the name in unison: Father bellowed it, Mother whispered it and Gwen repeated it flatly, not surprised in the least.

"You can understand my dilemma," Detective Sutter said. "He insists on what he saw."

"But he's lying," Gwen said.

"That's a strong statement," the detective intoned.

"How can he truthfully say he saw me being taken down the hall by anybody when I know it didn't happen that way?" The pounding in Gwen's head increased.

Father stood up. "There's one way to settle this. I'm going to find him and we'll all talk about this now. Together." He stalked from the room.

Gwen wasn't sure how she felt about this turn of events. On one hand, she truly didn't want to speak about something so personal with Charles in the room. On the other hand, the best way to bring the truth into the light was to speak in front of many witnesses. And there was no doubt in her mind that Charles was lying. The only question was, why?

Granted, he'd made his opinion of archery plain, and she knew he was no fan of Albert's. But would that be enough to accuse Albert of something so heinous? Could Charles truly go to such lengths just to sully the man's good name?

Time stretched out interminably as they waited for Father to return. When he finally did, Charles followed behind him, looking none too pleased to have been summoned.

Detective Sutter rose and held out his hand. "Mr. Drexler, good to see you again."

"You'll pardon me if I don't say likewise." Charles frowned, but still shook the man's hand. "What is this about?"

"Sir, there seems to be a discrepancy between your statement and that of Miss Banks."

Charles looked at her with an icy gaze. "That's no

surprise. Miss Banks suffered a head wound. She's just confused."

If one more person said Gwen was confused, she would scream. "Why would you say Mr. Taylor dragged me into that room when he didn't?"

"I can only tell you what I saw." Charles's voice had gone flat. "It's no wonder you don't want to remember it, after the way you've been throwing yourself at him."

Gwen reeled back as if he'd struck her.

Father took a step forward. "Watch yourself, young man."

"Actually, you should be watching your daughter, sir. It's shameful how she's been spending so much time with a common villager. Last night was the most disgraceful display of all."

Gwen got to her feet, reminding herself that committing murder would be a bad idea, given the presence of a police detective. "I did nothing improper last night, and neither did Albert. He never laid a hand on me."

"That's not how it looked when you were dancing with him."

Gwen's cheeks heated. How dare he take such a beautiful and important moment and make it sound cheap and illicit?

Mother clasped her hands to her chest. "Gwen, you danced? How did I miss that? That's wonderful."

"She danced with a villager," Charles spat out. "What's wonderful about that?" Then he turned his attention back to Gwen. "Why do you think he pays attention to you? Because he really cares about you? No, it's because he knows you're so desperate that you'll look past his low station. You think he's courting you, but it's just one more way he clutches at respectability, just like his quest for the competition."

Tears stung Gwen's eyes, and she couldn't hold them back. Charles was displaying his true colors, being petty and cruel. Nothing he said should hurt her, yet the words pelted her like hard, sharp rocks.

Detective Sutter moved forward, deflecting any more attempted verbal blows. "Mr. Drexler, you are displaying an obvious and somewhat irrational dislike for Mr. Taylor. It makes me wonder just how credible your testimony may be considered."

Charles pulled back his shoulders, making it appear that he looked down his nose at the detective, even though Charles was a good two inches shorter than the man. "I am a gentleman. My word stands."

"Still, Miss Banks, a well-respected woman of good character, has called your word false. As has Mr. Taylor. In fact, he claims it was you who told him exactly where to find Miss Banks, and how to get there." He turned to Gwen. "As you and I know, Miss Banks, it's quite a feat not getting lost in that house. It seems odd that Mr. Drexler would be able to give such detailed directions."

"Indeed it does." Gwen clenched her jaw.

"And then there's the testimony of Miss Matilda Banks." Detective Sutter shook his head before continuing. "She was most insistent that when she saw Mr. Taylor on his way *out* of the ballroom, he said that you had told him where to find her sister."

Charles remained silent as the detective continued on.

"The pieces are falling together and forming quite an interesting picture." Detective Sutter turned to Mr. Banks. "It's not common knowledge, but there have been several other robberies in the past few weeks, and all of them took place during parties. I'm leading the investigation, so I happen to know that Mr. Drexler was in attendance at each one of them."

"That doesn't prove anything," Charles said indignantly.

"No, it doesn't, not according to the statutes of the law. But it tells me to keep my eye on you."

Mr. Banks stepped forward. "This discourse has told me all I need to know, as well. Drexler, it would be best if you collected your things and left my home. Immediately."

Charles glowered at him through narrowed eyes. "Are you sure you want to do that? I'm still willing to make a respectable woman out of your daughter, despite her infirmity."

"How dare you," Gwen sputtered. "I wouldn't have you if my life depended on it."

"Let's hope it never comes to that," Charles replied.

"Jenkins!" A moment after Mr. Banks bellowed the name, a tall, neatly dressed butler hurried into the room.

"Yes, sir?"

"Mr. Drexler will be leaving us now, Jenkins. Please accompany him to his room and assist in his packing. I want to make quite sure that he doesn't get confused about which items belong to him."

"Understood, sir." Jenkins bowed slightly.

"And, Charles, you should start looking for new employment."

"You're firing me?" Charles asked, incredulous. "You can't do that. This has nothing to do with the quality of my work."

"Seeing as I own the company, I most certainly can

fire you. And that's exactly what I'm doing. Don't bother returning to the office. I'll have your desk cleared out and any personal belongings will be delivered to your home, along with your final week's pay." He made a shooing motion with one hand.

Charles glared from her father to Gwen and back again. Then he hurried from the room, with Jenkins right behind him.

Gwen thought there was something odd about Charles's reaction. Of course he would be upset over the loss of his job, but he had paled considerably when Father mentioned clearing out his desk. It was as if he was scared. Was there something in his desk he didn't want anyone to find? Did the secrets and mysteries surrounding this man never end? Charles liked to think that just because he worked in finance, he had a certain amount of class and respectability bred into him. But he didn't know what it meant to live a respectable life, not if lying came so easily to him.

Behind her, Detective Sutter was preparing to leave. "I should be on my way. I'm terribly sorry Drexler caused such an unpleasant scene, but I do believe his true nature has shown itself."

"Indeed." Father shook the detective's hand. "Does this mean Mr. Taylor is in the clear?"

Sutter shook his head. "No. I'm still conducting my investigation, though I expect to further clear Mr. Taylor. But there's still the complaint filed by the Ashfords. Unless that's withdrawn, Mr. Taylor is being charged with robbery."

The pain in Gwen's head intensified. How could she sit by idly while Albert was locked away in a cell?

What kind of conditions was he being forced to endure? "There has to be something we can do."

"I'll speak to William Ashford," Father said. "He's a sensible man. I'm sure I can make him understand the situation."

Relief flooded Gwen. One piece of the dilemma had been taken care of. Hopefully Matilda had been successful with hers.

Chapter 10

It had taken a bit of cajoling, but Gwen had finally gotten Mother to agree that some time out in the garden would do her good. It came with the caveat that Gwen would sit on a bench, in the shade, and promise not to dig for insects or follow any animals. It was all perfectly fine with Gwen. Her plan was to sit there and wait for Matilda to come back with news.

Detective Sutter had said he would continue his investigation. Gwen assumed that would include a visit to Albert's home, if he hadn't been there already. What would he find? Had Matilda discovered anything? Or was this whole scenario with secret codes and hidden messages just something she and Matilda had created in their minds?

What if they'd gone for all this trouble simply to feed a cat?

"Psst!" The hissing of someone trying to get her attention caught Gwen's ear. She looked to her left and there was Matilda, leaning out from behind the trunk of a very flimsy tree. The fact that no one, not even Matilda, could possibly expect to be hidden from view behind it might have made the sight comical, if not for the cross look on Matilda's face.

"Matilda, you're—"

Matilda held up her hand to halt Gwen's words, and then she motioned quickly for Gwen to follow her.

Mother would be livid if she came back and found Gwen gone, but that couldn't be helped now. She slowly pushed herself up from the bench and followed Matilda out of the garden. When they'd gotten what she considered a safe distance from the house, Gwen called after her.

"Are you going to tell me what happened?"

Matilda slowed down a bit to allow Gwen to catch up, but she didn't stop moving. "Oh, my…where to begin? As I expected, Jason was more than happy to lend his assistance. We went to the clubhouse and found the groom you told me about. He didn't know where Albert lived, but he was able to point us toward someone who did."

She wasn't sure how she felt about involving more people in their mission. "What reason did you give for needing his address?"

"I told them I had to look after his cat." Matilda threw up her hands in frustration as she stomped over the uneven ground. "What else could I say? At that point, I didn't know what I was going to find."

That had an ominous sound to it. "I take it you and Jason found his home, then?"

"Yes, we did."

"And?"

"And…well, there was a cat."

Gwen's heart clenched. "Really? We really did all this in order to feed the man's cat?"

"No, not exactly. There was a cat there, yes, but we found something else, too."

She waited for Matilda to explain, but her sister just kept walking. Finally, Gwen couldn't take it. "Tilda, please stop and tell me what happened. What did you find?"

When Matilda turned around, she was chewing on her bottom lip, a rather unladylike habit that popped up whenever she was nervous. "I'd rather not say just yet. It's complicated, and I'm not entirely sure I understand it myself. I think it's something you need to see."

"Can you at least tell me where we're going?"

She pointed down the path. "The caretaker's shed. It was the first private place I could think of."

Matilda continued walking and Gwen followed. What could be so terrible that Matilda couldn't tell her about it? Whatever it was, she would find out soon.

Jason Adler's automobile was parked beside the shed. Matilda rapped on the door. "Jason! It's Matilda. I've got Gwen with me."

The door cracked open just enough for Jason to peer out. "It's about time. I don't know how much longer this is going to work."

"I appreciate your help. I promise you, I won't forget this."

Any other day, Gwen would have taken note of Matilda's smile and come to the conclusion that her sister had more than a passing fancy for Mr. Adler. But today was not that kind of day.

Gwen put her hand on Matilda's shoulder. "Why don't we go inside and you can tell me everything?"

"All right, but brace yourself. Remember, I told you we found a cat?"

"Yes."

"Well, we found something else. Rather, we found *someone* else."

"Rachel," Jason piped up. "We found Rachel."

He pushed open the shed door, and Gwen took a careful step inside. A young woman sat on a short stool against the back wall. She was hunched over a cat that she held tightly in her lap, and she rocked ever so slightly. Her black hair had been put into a thick braid, but large pieces of it had come loose and hung around her face.

Gwen's blood ran cold as she looked down at the forlorn woman in front of her. Who was she to Albert, and why was she at his home? "I don't understand."

"Neither do we," Matilda said. "She doesn't talk much. All she would say is that her name is Rachel and the cat is Mr. Mittens."

"And she trusts Albert," Jason added. "She wouldn't stop screaming until we told her that Albert had sent us to her."

Matilda nodded. "And that's the only reason she came with us this far. But I think she expected Albert to be here."

The young woman made a whimpering sound at the mention of his name. When she looked up, her gray eyes were round with fear, her face filthy as if smeared with soot from the fireplace. "Where is Albert?"

"He's had a bit of trouble," Gwen said gently. "But he asked us to take care of you until he can come back home."

Matilda stepped up to Gwen's side. "We can't keep the poor thing out here in the shed," she whispered. "What do we do now?"

"Somehow, we've got to find a way to get her into my room." Gwen turned her attention back to Rachel. "Would you like to see my room? We can get you cleaned up, and if you like, I can brush your hair for you."

Something sparked in her eyes, and a hint of a smile showed beneath the grime. "Albert brushes my hair. I love that."

Gwen would brush her hair all day if that's what it took to keep the young woman quiet. "It's settled, then." She looked up at Matilda. "You know what we need now."

Matilda nodded. "Another distraction."

"We have to get everybody as far away from the staircase as possible."

"Leave that to me," Jason said. "I know the perfect way to empty a house."

Before Gwen could ask what he meant, Jason left the shed and started his automobile. When he drove away, Gwen looked at Matilda in disbelief. "He's not doing what I think he's doing, is he?"

"I'm fairly certain he is," Matilda said.

The sound of the automobile chugging away broke the tranquility of the morning, and a minute later, a loud crash followed by the shouts of many people confirmed their suspicions: Jason had purposely wrecked his automobile in front of the Banks house.

"Come on, we'd best hurry." Gwen put a hand on Rachel's arm. "Will you come with us, dear?"

The promise of hair brushing had made Rachel much more compliant. She nodded her head and stood up, still clutching Mr. Mittens to her chest. The poor cat complained and squirmed, scratching at Rachel's hands, although the woman didn't seem to notice. In fact, her hands were covered with scratch marks, some partially healed, some brand-new. It would be a marvel if they could get both Rachel and the cat into the house with no one seeing.

Of course, she didn't expect to keep Rachel a secret forever. But she needed time to figure out why Albert would keep a woman at his house and not tell anyone about her.

And she needed to figure out exactly how she felt about that.

There were worse things than being in solitary confinement. Sharing a cell with a man who called himself Bartholomew the Butcher had turned out to be one of them.

It had taken precisely one hour after the time the Butcher was put in the holding cell for the thug to attack Albert. It seemed the notion of a villager hobnobbing with the social upper crust rankled with the common man, too. And the Butcher was the most common of common men. Now Albert's aching ribs were tightly bound and he lay on a rough cot, surrounded by the silence of solitary where he'd been moved for his own protection.

But what was there left to protect? His dreams for the competition lay in a shambles at his feet. Even if he could still find someone who wanted to sponsor him, what kind of an archer would he be after his arm healed? And what of Gwen? Did she believe in his innocence? Or had Charles Drexler convinced her that he was nothing but a ne'er-do-well who wanted to take advantage of her and hurt her?

Albert threw an arm over his eyes, immersing himself in a darkness that matched the feeling in his soul. They said that when God closed a door, somewhere he opened a window, but Albert was starting to doubt it. All he saw was a cell with not a window in sight.

The sound of singing floated to him from the other side of the wall. Curious, Albert pressed his ear against the wood, straining to make out the words. It sounded like the fellow was singing the same lines over and over. Finally, Albert was able to make them out.

When peace like a river, attendeth my way,
When sorrows like sea billows roll;
Whatever my lot, Thou hast taught me to say,
It is well, it is well, with my soul.

Albert rolled over and sat up. He was familiar with the hymn, written by a man who had lost almost everything and everyone that mattered in his life. He'd always wondered how someone could reach such a low state and still hold such unshakable faith. Now here he was, in a state lower than he'd ever experienced in his life, and it began to make sense.

The decision was his. God had not left him, nor would He ever leave him. But it was Albert's decision whether or not to acknowledge God's kingship in his life, and more important, to trust in it.

The door at the end of the short corridor opened and in walked Detective Sutter. He stood outside the small cell door and shook his head. "I can't believe they put a brute like that in your cell. How are you feeling?"

"The doctor thinks the ribs are just bruised, maybe cracked. They should heal well," Albert said. "Please tell me you've come with good news."

Sutter seesawed his hand back and forth. "It depends how you look at it. I certainly think things are looking up for you. Charles Drexler, on the other hand, well, let's just say I wouldn't want to be him."

The detective gave Albert a quick rundown of his visit to the Bankses' home. It was all he could do to hold in his rage when he heard how cruelly the cad had spoken to Gwen. But he took heart when he discovered that Mr. Banks had thrown him out.

"Then Mr. Banks believes in my innocence?"

Sutter nodded. "Indeed he does. He also promised to speak to Mr. Ashford about withdrawing the robbery charge. Once that's done, you're a free man."

"Thank the good Lord in Heaven. And thank you, Detective."

"I'm simply doing my job."

"I don't know about that. It seems you've gone out of your way to look at the facts when you could have just taken the word of some very well-connected men." Albert grinned. "I'm tempted to think of you as my own personal guardian angel."

An incredulous laugh burst from Sutter's lips. "I've been called many things, but I've never been called an angel. Now, let me give you one more word of advice. When they let you out of here, keep your eyes open for Drexler. He's angry and he's been wounded, which makes him dangerous. I'm afraid he may try to take revenge on you or Miss Banks."

Albert leaned forward on the cot. "Is Gwen in any danger?"

"Right now, no. Not as long as she's home with her family. But as I told them, I recommend that someone is with her at all times. If you'll excuse me, I have work to attend to."

As Detective Sutter walked down the hall, he began to hum. And before the door shut behind him, Albert caught a few sung words.

"It is well with my soul."

It had been a long afternoon. Once Matilda and Gwen got Rachel upstairs, they started by getting her cleaned up. Convincing her to put the cat down had proven nearly impossible, until Matilda hit on the magic phrase: *let's do it for Albert.*

"Let's get you cleaned up for Albert," Matilda had said. "Won't that be nice?"

Rachel blinked at her, then nodded. "Yes. Albert likes it when I'm clean and neat."

As soon as Mr. Mittens was released, the cat dove for safety beneath the bed. Rachel was smaller than Gwen, but one of the dresses she used for her nature walks would do just fine. After Matilda had helped her with a sponge bath, and Gwen assisted her dressing, it was time to deal with her hair.

They soon discovered that Rachel loved having her hair tended to, but only until the brush encountered a tangle or a knot. One pull on her hair elicited howls of pain disproportionate to the situation. More than once, Gwen had to use the special phrase.

"Let's do this for Albert. Won't he love seeing how pretty and silky your hair is?"

And then Rachel would answer, each word like a knife to Gwen's heart. "Albert brushes my hair every night. One hundred strokes."

"It sounds like Albert takes very good care of you," Matilda said.

"Oh, yes. He tells me what to do to stay safe. And he says I must never say too much about myself to anyone, and I must not talk at all to strangers. But you aren't strangers because you know Albert."

"That's right," Gwen agreed. And since they were talking about Albert, maybe now was a good time to do a little fishing. "How long have you known Albert?"

"A very long time." She shook her head sharply, almost pulling the hair brush from Gwen's hand. "But he doesn't like me to talk about that."

Another dead end. Gwen continued brushing in silence.

After Rachel's hair was brushed, falling down her back in a dark, silken cascade, she had a particularly chatty moment.

"I love to dance. Albert has been teaching me. He says I am beautiful and that he's never seen anyone as graceful as I am."

Then she moved around the room, twirling and dipping, holding her arms out as if they were around an imaginary partner. Gwen's imagination filled in the empty space, saw Albert dancing with her. Rachel was indeed graceful, far more so than Gwen could ever hope to be.

Finally, Gwen was able to convince Rachel to lie down. Despite her protests that she couldn't sleep until she'd seen Albert, she was softly snoring not five minutes after her head settled onto the pillow.

"Well," Gwen whispered. "What do you suppose we've gotten ourselves into?"

Matilda sank into a chair and shook her head. "It would help if we knew who she was. You don't suppose..."

Matilda didn't have to finish her sentence for Gwen to know what she was thinking. "That she's his wife? I don't know."

Was Albert like Mr. Rochester, the tortured hero of *Jane Eyre*, who kept his insane wife locked away from prying eyes? The thought that Albert could so thoroughly deceive her was a pain too great to bear. He obviously cared enough about Rachel that he had seen to her welfare, even though doing so effectively gave away his secret. Should she admire him for that, or did his lies of omission reveal his true character? There was only one thing Gwen could think to do now.

"Matilda, would you mind staying with her for a bit? I need to talk to Father."

Father had a massive desk in his study, positioned so that it was the first thing anyone who walked in would see. When he sat behind it, he looked rather like Gwen imagined the president of the United States would look. But when she found him in his study, he wasn't sitting behind the desk. He stood at the window, hands stuffed in his trouser pockets, staring through the glass.

"Father, are you all right?"

He didn't turn around. "We come here every summer to enjoy ourselves, but I spend so much time inside, thinking about work and politics and things that don't really matter, that I never really experience nature. Not like you do. I thought at least I should try to look at it. But there are streaks on the glass." He pointed to the window. "It keeps you from truly seeing the beauty that's there."

She wasn't sure what Father was getting at, so she let him continue.

"I owe you an apology, Gwen."

"Me? Why?"

"I haven't seen you for who you really are. I'm ashamed to say, I let the fact that you have a clubfoot impair my judgment. You're a strong, capable, amazing woman. I see that now. But I thought you needed my help to be happy."

Gwen stepped directly behind him and put her hand on his shoulder. "It's all right, Father. You meant well."

"Good intentions and all that." Father turned to face her. His eyes were red, and tears threatened to fall. "I never should have brought Charles here. What madness made me think you and he would be a good match?"

Gwen couldn't help but laugh. "Truly, I've asked myself that same question a few times."

Father tried to smile in return, but his expression remained sad. "You deserve so much better. You deserve someone who appreciates your intelligence and your talent."

Receiving compliments from Father should have filled her with pride. Instead, she felt like a sham. When he found out about Rachel, and how Albert had kept her a secret, he'd know that Gwen was just as easily fooled as anyone else.

"Father, there's something I need to tell you. And I need your advice."

He looked surprised. "Of course."

As she told him the story, he remained silent, although he crossed his arms over his chest when she told him about sneaking Rachel up to her room.

When she finished, he considered her words, then sighed deeply. "Is that why young Mr. Adler ran his automobile into the statue up front? To cause a distraction?"

Gwen hung her head. "Yes, Father."

"Humph. Remind me to thank him the next time I see him. I've never liked that thing, but your mother refused to let me replace it. Now we have no choice." He put a finger beneath Gwen's chin and lifted her head so they were eye to eye. "This doesn't mean I'm not cross with you for deceiving me, but I certainly understand your motives."

With a gulp, Gwen gave a little nod. "Thank you."

"And now, we must figure out what to do about exonerating Mr. Taylor and caring for the woman who is resting upstairs."

"You mean, you're still willing to speak to Mr. Ashford on Albert's behalf?" Gwen had been certain her father would rescind his offer once she told him everything.

"Of course. Unless you've changed your mind about his innocence."

"Oh, no. I'm absolutely sure Albert did not assault me, nor did he commit the robbery."

"Then we must do what we can to clear his name, regardless." Father scratched his chin absently. "I must say, the fact that he made sure you would be able to find this woman and care for her reflects well on his character. Rather than leave her to fend for herself, he revealed his secret. That leads me to believe he must have had a good reason for the secret in the first place."

She hadn't considered it in that way. Her heart lightened just a bit. "I do hope so, Father."

"Well, there's only one way for us to find out." He motioned for Gwen to lead the way out of his office.

As she walked up the stairs to her room, Father right behind her, Gwen uttered a silent prayer.

Please, Lord, let there be a reason that makes sense.

Chapter 11

Albert had been sitting in the interrogation room for an undetermined length of time. There was no clock on the wall, and his pocket watch had been taken with the rest of his belongings. If someone had asked him how long it had been, he wouldn't be able to say. Time seemed to have slowed to a near standstill since the police locked him away.

The door finally opened. Albert wasn't surprised when Detective Sutter walked in. What did surprise him was that Gwen's father was right behind him.

Albert shot to his feet. "Detective. Mr. Banks. Is Gwen all right?"

Mr. Banks didn't speak, didn't blink. The detective motioned quickly with his hand. "Miss Banks is just fine. I saw her myself yesterday. Mr. Banks was able to speak to Mr. Ashford and convince him to withdraw the complaint."

Albert could barely believe he was hearing correctly. "Does that mean I'm free to go?"

"Yes and no." Detective Sutter motioned to the chair. "Please, sit back down." After Albert sat, the detective continued. "Mr. Banks asked to speak to you privately before your release. Since he was instrumental in your exoneration, I didn't think you'd be opposed to it."

"Of course not," Albert said.

"Wonderful. Mr. Banks, have a seat. I'll leave the door unlocked and wait in the hall until you're finished." The detective left the room.

Mr. Banks pulled out the other chair and settled himself across from Albert. Then he planted his elbows on the table, clasped his hands together and leaned forward.

"Mr. Taylor, the most important thing in my life is my family. You should know that anyone who hurts either of my daughters is opening himself up for a world of hurt. Are we clear?"

The look on Mr. Banks's face made the Butcher seem like a happy man. "Yes, sir."

"Good." He leaned back and relaxed a bit. "Rachel is at my home."

Tears pricked at Albert's eyes. It would never do to cry in front of this formidable man, but the sense of relief was overwhelming. "Is she all right?"

Mr. Banks nodded. "She's confused, but physically she's fine. So is your cat, by the way."

"The cat?"

"Yes. Rachel wouldn't leave the house without him."

Of course not. Mr. Mittens could have fended for himself indefinitely, but Rachel couldn't do without the feline. "Thank you."

"Now for the most important question. Who is she?"

Albert tilted his head in confusion. "She didn't tell you?"

"No, the girl is quite closemouthed when it comes to specific details about who she is. Although we did find out that she loves to dance and to have her hair brushed. And of course, she loves that cat."

It wasn't a laughing matter, but Albert still allowed himself a chuckle. So Rachel had listened to some of the warnings he'd given her. The frown that pulled down on Mr. Banks's mustache reminded him to be serious.

"I'm sorry, sir. Rachel is my sister."

His eyebrows lifting, Mr. Banks leaned forward once more. "Your sister? Well, that is good news. I was afraid we might have had a Mr. Rochester on our hands."

Albert flushed at the implication. "No, sir, I would never do a thing like that."

"Yet you've chosen to keep your sister a secret. I'm curious as to why."

They'd met Rachel. He'd have thought it would be obvious. "Rachel has a disease which affects her body as well as her mind. When Rachel was young, she had seizures, terrible shaking fits that would leave her unable to function for days."

"I'm sorry," Mr. Banks said with a sympathetic frown. "Does she still experience the seizures?"

"No, she hasn't had one of those for years. But her mind has been affected. In many ways, she's more like a child than a woman."

"And that's why you keep her hidden? Because she embarrasses you?"

The judgment fell hard on Albert. It was something he'd long ago admitted to himself, but still a fact he despised. "That's part of it, yes, sir. But there's a bigger reason. When Rachel is out in public, there's no telling how she will act. She has been treated very badly by small-minded people who don't understand her issues. I've kept Rachel hidden to protect us both."

Mr. Banks took a moment to digest the information, looking down at his hands as he clasped and unclasped his fingers. Then, he slowly looked up at Albert.

"I'd like to say if I was in your position, I'd do the same thing. But I can't."

Shame burned in Albert as Mr. Banks stood up and walked around the table. Of course this man of class and status would have handled the situation differently.

Mr. Banks clasped Albert on the shoulder. "No, if it were me, I would have put her in a home and washed my hands of the problem. You are a better man than I, son."

"Sir?" Confusion and relief warred in Albert's head.

"Gwen was right. You are a man of good character."

"Then Gwen isn't upset with me?"

"Oh, I didn't say that." Mr. Banks puffed out a laugh. "She's about as upset as you'd expect. Remember, she doesn't know what you just told me. All she knows is that you lied to her."

That was true. He'd never intentionally lied, but he'd held back the truth. It was still a betrayal of her trust. "Do you think she'll forgive me?"

"I'd like to think so, but I gave up trying to understand women years ago. As much as I'd like to help you, you're on your own with Gwen. But I can do this." He held his hand out. "You have my blessing."

Gwen was not going to make this easy. When he'd gone to the Bankses' home to collect Rachel, Gwen had been nowhere in sight. Instead, he found Matilda sitting on the porch with Rachel, who held Mr. Mittens in a death grip. When Albert asked if he could speak to Gwen, Matilda shook her head.

"I'm sorry, Albert. She told me to tell you she's not ready to see you." She looked as though she hated delivering the message. "I think she's still recovering from her head injury. It's making her moody."

While it was sweet of Matilda to try and spare his feelings, he understood all too well. Gwen needed time, and he had no choice but to give it to her.

Rachel, on the other hand, was less understanding. She appeared to have bonded with Gwen. Even after he got her settled in back at home, she chattered on and on about her new friend.

"When will we see Gwen? She was so nice to me. And she brushed my hair without hurting my head hardly at all."

Well, of course she did. Gwen was a woman and knew how to do womanly things like brushing long, prone-to-tangling hair. He'd been caring for Rachel for ten years, and he still couldn't do it without sending his poor sister into tears.

That night, Rachel would only go to sleep with the promise that he would invite Gwen over for a visit soon. As he lay in bed, sleep stayed far out of his reach. Instead, he wondered if Gwen would show up for her archery lessons that week, or if those were over now, too.

The next day, he realized that Gwen wasn't the only one he had to worry about. Out of the six lessons he had scheduled, only two showed up. One of them was Grenville Kane.

"Mr. Kane, I'm glad to see you." Albert approached with a smile, but it didn't stay in place for long.

"I'm afraid I don't come with tidings of great joy."

The man didn't have to go into detail for Albert to know what came next. "I'm not going to the games, am I?"

"I'm afraid not," Mr. Kane grumbled. "As far as I'm concerned, there's no issue. You were exonerated. All the charges were dropped. But there are others who feel that the lingering memory of this ordeal will taint the name of the Tuxedo Club. They won't put their influence, or their money, behind you."

Albert wanted to argue that not only had he not done anything wrong, but he was a victim, too. He'd been framed, and by a Parkie. But perhaps that was part of the problem. They wouldn't want to admit that one of their own could act in such a way. They'd rather ignore the situation altogether and let it die from lack of attention.

So, instead of arguing, Albert responded in the only way he knew how. "Thank you for coming to tell me in person, Mr. Kane. I appreciate your kindness."

Mr. Kane slapped him on the back. "It's the least I can do, young man."

Then the man walked away, taking a good portion of Albert's dreams with him.

"Gwen! Are you out here?"

Hunkered down behind a tree, Gwen wondered what would happen if she just didn't answer. It was highly unlikely Matilda would venture off the path. Still, her sister always had the capacity to surprise her. And given the unwanted excitement they'd had lately, it probably wasn't a good idea to hide from her.

"I'm over here."

Gwen rose slowly and looked down the path.

"There you are." Matilda stomped over to her, holding up her skirts to keep the hem out of the dirt. "Mother has been going out of her mind."

Gwen blew out an exasperated sigh. "I told her I was going for a walk, just like I've done every other day this week. What is she worried about?"

"That's just it. You've been in the same area every day. Haven't you run out of stuff to put in your journal?"

"That's the great thing about nature. You can go to the same spot over and over again, and you'll always find something different." She opened her journal. "See, I drew this yesterday, but today—"

"Stop. No more." Matilda was having none of it. "Why have you stopped taking archery lessons?"

Gwen shrugged. "Because I've learned all I need to. There aren't that many different ways to nock an arrow and pull back on the bowstring."

"So it has nothing to do with Albert?"

"No."

"You're not trying to punish him?"

"Punish him?" It was a ridiculous thought. "Why would I want to punish him?"

Matilda raised a hand and pulled back one finger. "Because he lied to you." She pulled back another. "Because he hurt your feelings." And another. "Because you're in love with him and that scares you to death."

"Enough." Gwen stopped her before she could go any further. "I'm not trying to punish him. But yes, I am hurt. And I can't get over the way he treated his sister."

"What did he do to her? From what I can see he

took care of her and made sure she had everything she needed."

"He hid her away, Tilda. He kept her a secret."

"But he did that for her own good. To protect her."

"Because of her illness. Because she doesn't always act the right way around people, and she could have a seizure." Gwen's throat felt thick and she could barely get the words out. "He's afraid of how she'll look in public."

"Gwenie, that's not the same as you." Matilda put a gentle hand on her arm. "How many times have you been in public with Albert? For goodness' sakes, the man wouldn't leave you alone until you danced with him. That's not how a man acts if he's embarrassed to be seen with you."

"Maybe Charles was right. Maybe he just did all that to enhance his social status."

"Charles? You'd take the words of that worm over the facts told to you by your loving sister?" Matilda clucked her tongue. "That blow to your head must have done more damage than we thought."

Gwen laughed out loud. Matilda was right. She was being ridiculous, overreacting and not giving Albert a chance to defend himself. Perhaps she was punishing him, or she was simply working extremely hard to spin a protective cocoon around herself. Either way, it was time to stop.

"When did you become so smart, little sister?"

Matilda shrugged. "When you weren't looking, I suppose. Does this mean you're ready to face the world again?"

Gwen pulled her shoulders back. "Yes. What would you say to the Banks girls making a visit to the clubhouse?"

"I'd say it's about time." Matilda giggled and held out her arm. "Shall we?"

Gwen threaded her arm through Matilda's "Absolutely."

If Gwen had felt on display before, this visit to the clubhouse made her feel like a spectacle. She could barely walk five feet without someone asking her how she felt, telling her they were at the Ashfords' that night or expressing their disdain at the spate of robberies that had finally been made common knowledge.

Mrs. Fitzsimmons was particularly vocal. "What's the world coming to when good people can't open their homes without some villager slipping in to rob them blind?"

Gwen would have none of it. "I'm sure you're mistaken. Albert Taylor was exonerated of all wrongdoing and the charges dropped. In fact, it's come to light that suspicion was thrown his way by the prime suspect, who is a member of the upper class."

Before the woman could reply, Gwen and Matilda moved along.

"Oh, dear." Matilda held her side as she tried not to laugh out loud. "Did you see how her mouth hung open like a codfish? I believe you set the record straight, Gwenie."

"I just hope she spreads the facts as ably as she spreads gossip."

They continued to the archery range. It was full of people aiming at targets, some on their own and some accompanied by instructors. Gwen looked from one end of the line to the other, then looked again.

"I don't see Albert."

"Maybe he wasn't scheduled to work today," Matilda suggested.

"No, this is one of his normal days." Gwen spotted another instructor that had seemed to be a friend of Albert's. "Come on. Let's find out where he is."

They approached the man, standing back as he gave instructions to a lovely woman with golden hair and, Gwen noted, a perfect stance.

"Very good, Gladys. I think this new bow will work even better for you. Give it a try."

As the woman proceeded, he moved to Gwen and Matilda. "Very nice to see you again, Miss Banks."

So he remembered her. If only she could recall his name. "Likewise. This is my sister, Matilda."

He bowed slightly. "A pleasure. I'm Jonah Walker." Matilda nodded in response. Once the pleasantries were done, Jonah got to the point. "How can I help you ladies?"

"We're looking for Albert Taylor," Gwen said.

His well-practiced look of pleasant respect was slightly marred by a wrinkling of his forehead. "I'm afraid Albert is no longer employed here."

"Did he quit?"

"No, ma'am. He was informed his services were no longer required."

Gwen was struck speechless. Matilda, however, had more than enough words for both of them.

"How could they do that? Albert had nothing to do with the assault, or the robbery. He was cleared of all those charges. This is a travesty!"

"Matilda, please." Gwen grabbed her sister's wrist. "Making a scene won't help anyone."

Jonah looked around quickly, then leaned closer.

"The one thing that might help is proving who really committed the crimes." He kept his voice low.

"But the police have a suspect," Gwen answered.

"Yes, but they're short on hard evidence." At her questioning look, he gave a shrug. "I have a friend in the police department."

"Thank you, Mr. Walker. I appreciate your candor."

"In that case—" Jonah glanced around again before continuing "—most of the Parkies treat us like we're not worth their time, unless they need us for something. But you've never been that way. And I know Albert respects you. He's my friend, and I think he deserves something good in his life. I think you do, too."

Yes, that was indeed a candid response. "Thank you again. We should really be going now."

"This is terrible," Matilda said as they walked away. "What are we going to do?"

"You heard him. The only way to help Albert is to find proof that leads to the arrest of the real criminal." Gwen was positive she knew who that person was. If only there was a way to prove it.

From the corner of her eye, Gwen saw someone moving quickly toward them. She braced herself for another inane comment by someone who didn't care about facts, but was relieved to see a friendly face.

"Mr. Adler, it's so good to see you." Gwen reached out and squeezed his wrist. "I haven't had the opportunity to thank you for all your help the other day."

A faint blush crept up from under Jason's shirt collar. "Don't mention it, miss. I was happy to do it."

"No, it was the act of a true friend. And my father sends his thanks, as well."

Now Jason smiled. "I received a message from Mr.

Banks in that regard. Something about how I saved him the trouble of having the statue removed. He even offered to pay for the repairs to my automobile."

"That's wonderful," Matilda said.

"Yes, quite. But I wanted to talk to you both about something else." His voice dropped into a conspiratorial tone. "Drexler is here."

"Charles?" Gwen scanned the grounds but didn't see the man. "Where?"

"I saw him over there." He pointed in the direction of the tennis courts. "And he was with Odette Pettibone."

Matilda gaped at the discovery. "Why would he be with Odette?"

"I don't know," Jason said with a shrug. "It makes no sense."

Gwen gave her head a hard shake. "No, it makes perfect sense."

Matilda nudged her arm. "Would you care to explain it to us?"

Oh, she really didn't want to. There was no way to explain it without sounding like she was passing judgment on others, but they had to get to the bottom of the situation.

"Tilda, you told me once how Charles loved meeting new people. And at the balls, remember how he always danced with the other girls? The ones that usually don't spend much time dancing?"

Matilda nodded. "Yes. He made a point of it. He even said to me once that even the wallflowers deserved some attention."

Gwen cringed thinking of how Charles may have used those women. "I think his purpose was to get close to the women in order to steal from them."

"Wait a minute. Drexler?" Jason's voice grew louder. "We think Drexler is the robber?"

"Shh!" Both the sisters hissed at him at the same time.

Matilda swatted his arm. "You already know that. He's the one who set up Albert."

"Yes, I know *that*." Jason waggled his head from side to side. "But you think he committed all those other robberies, too?"

"Yes," they spoke together again.

Jason let out a long, low whistle. "This just gets worse and worse."

"I wouldn't be surprised if Charles talked his way into the Pettibone home, and he's staying with them now," Gwen continued.

"This is dreadful," Matilda said. "How are we ever to prove what he's up to?"

"I'm not sure, but first things first."

Gwen had to get a message to Albert. She had to apologize for refusing to see him after all he'd gone through. After that, they could work together to expose Charles for the criminal he was. And then hopefully Gwen and Albert could discover if there was any future for them beyond the archery range.

Chapter 12

For the first time since they'd begun summering in Tuxedo Park, the Banks family was holding a ball. It had never seemed practical before, given Gwen's aversion to crowds and dancing, but now, everything was different. Now they had more than just a social reason for holding such a gala event.

Gwen and Matilda had formulated the plan as they returned home from the clubhouse. They'd shared it with their father, who gave his blessing. The only member of the family who didn't know was Mrs. Banks, who would surely put an end to it if she learned the true purpose of the ball. Instead she'd spent the past two days happily preparing for guests.

Now those guests were arriving.

Matilda and Gwen stood together near the entrance of the ballroom, watching each person who came in.

So far, the people they most wanted to see hadn't arrived.

"They're not coming," Matilda whispered. "Neither one will come, and this will be a huge waste of time."

Gwen put a calming hand on her sister's back. "They will come. I'm sure of it."

Ten minutes later, Gwen accepted a glass of punch from one of the servers and began to doubt her earlier conviction. Neither man really had a concrete reason to show up, save the ones that Gwen had conjured in her own imagination.

Then, she turned her head and there he was. The first unknowing participant in their plan.

Just as Gwen expected, Charles entered the room with Odette Pettibone on his arm. The girl's eyes were huge as she looked around. Gwen couldn't recall seeing her escorted to any of the other parties. This was surely a new and heady experience for Odette. The idea that it was all a sham, that Charles was using her as a means to an end, made Gwen ache for her.

Gwen leaned over and whispered, "Charles is here. Remember, we invited him and we're glad to see him."

"I remember." Matilda moved away from Gwen, gliding across the floor to meet the couple. "Charles! Odette! I'm so glad you both could come. And, Odette, your dress is stunning." Matilda took her hands and gave them a squeeze.

Her dress truly was beautiful. And the smile that lit Odette's face at the compliment almost made her beautiful, too.

"Thank you so much for the invitation," Odette said.

"Yes, it was gladly received, although a bit unexpected," Charles said. "Odette, would you be a dear and fetch me a glass of punch?"

Odette almost jumped up and down at the prospect of doing something for him. "Oh yes, of course." And she scurried off.

Gwen now stood beside Matilda. "Good evening, Charles." She held out her hand.

"Gwen." He took her hand in his, bowing slightly over her fingers, then immediately let go. "I hope this means there are no hard feelings between us."

"It means that the past holds little interest for me. All I want to concentrate on now is the future."

"A very healthy attitude." He grinned in a way that reminded her of a garden snake just before it swallowed up a cricket.

"Oh, dear!" Matilda gasped and clutched at the front of her dress.

"What happened?" Gwen asked.

"I almost lost this." She held out her hand, revealing a beautiful diamond-and-sapphire necklace. "The clasp must have broken."

"I told you not to wear that tonight. Mother would be apoplectic if you lost it. Come on, let's put it in Father's office safe."

"We don't know the combination."

"Fine, then we'll just put it in his desk." Gwen turned back to Charles. "Please excuse us."

"Of course."

It wasn't until the sisters reached the office and shut the door that they allowed themselves to breathe freely.

Matilda gasped and fell into the chair behind Father's desk. "Do you think he believed us?"

"I'm not sure. At any rate, we've baited the trap the best we can." Now to see if the rat would bite.

Albert held his head high as he walked into the Banks home. He no longer wore a fine tuxedo; he had returned that to Mr. Kane, not feeling right about keeping it. Instead, he wore the best—and only—suit he owned. It was at least several seasons out of fashion, but it was dark and clean. He was determined that from here on out, people would have to see him for who he was. If that wasn't good enough for them, then so be it.

"Albert, my good man." Mr. Banks strode up to him and welcomed him with a hearty handshake. "So glad you could make it."

"Thank you for the invitation, sir." Albert tried to casually look beyond Mr. Banks, but the man caught on right away.

"Yes, Gwen is here," he said with a chuckle. "And yes, she knows you've been invited. Now go and enjoy the party."

"Thank you, sir."

Mr. Banks walked on to converse with more guests, while Albert moved deeper into the throng. The ballroom at the Bankses' home was modest in comparison to some of the others he'd seen, but it struck him as a perfect representation of the family. Well-appointed, yes, but not flaunting itself.

A small orchestra was playing, several couples were dancing, but Albert didn't see Gwen anywhere. Then a thought occurred to him. He made his way across the room to a set of tall French doors that led outside. The garden was beautiful in the moonlight, as was the woman who stood a few feet away, looking up at a tree.

"Gwen."

She turned so quickly that her foot caught in the train of her dress, causing her to wobble. Albert reached out for her elbow to steady her.

Gwen flushed, her lashes dipping slightly. "It seems you're always coming to my rescue."

"And now you're coming to mine." He appreciated that she didn't deny the fact. "You're trying to help me regain a place in society. I'm not sure how important that is anymore, but I thank you for the thought."

Gwen shook her head. "It's not that simple. This is also about clearing your good name once and for all."

"You'd think being found innocent of all charges would have done that."

"Yes, well, the only way to stop the speculation about you is to prove who really did it."

Albert was confused. "How will attending a party do that?"

"We have a plan."

"We?"

"Matilda, Jason and I."

"Jason? Jason Adler? The young man who can't keep his automobile on the road?"

"Well, yes," Gwen said, narrowing her eyes a bit. "But he does have attributes other than that. He helped us find Rachel, you know."

"Actually, no, I didn't realize that. I'll have to thank him."

Gwen looked past Albert. "You didn't bring her with you, did you?"

"No."

"You need to bring her out into public," Gwen said. "It's not fair to hide her away."

"I know, but this is the wrong event to start with."
Rachel loved the idea of going to a ball but the reality
would be so much more difficult to deal with. "There
are too many people, too many new things all at once.
We need to start smaller."

"As long as you start." Her voice was so soft, it was
nearly a whisper.

He didn't want to spend the evening talking about
Charles and Rachel. He wanted to talk about Gwen.
"What were you looking at when I came out?"

A smile grew on her lips. "There just so happens to
be one of nature's masterpieces right there in that tree.
Take a look."

Albert stepped closer and looked up at where she was
pointing. There, in the V between the tree trunk and a
branch, a spider had spun its web. The delicate fibers
glowed in the moonlight, twinkling as they swayed in
the gentle breeze.

"You were right," he said. "It's a beautiful sight."

She was a beautiful sight. There she was in the most
simple ball gown he'd seen her wear, yet she outshone
every other woman in the place. He expected she'd
made her choice because she knew he'd arrive in more
common attire, and she meant for him to be comfortable. Her kindness only made him love her more.

"Gwen, I'm so sorry I hurt you."

She looked up at him, and for a moment, the betrayal
in her eyes was palpable. "Yes, I was hurt. But I understand why you chose not to tell me about your sister.
I accept your apology, but only if you accept mine."

"Yours?" Albert tilted his head slightly. "You have
nothing to apologize for."

"Oh yes, I do. I refused to see you, even after I knew

the truth about Rachel." She sighed and shook her head. "It was wrong of me to turn away from you when you needed me most. I—"

Albert put a finger to her lips, cutting her sentence short. "That's quite enough. You're forgiven. Now, I think we have more important, and more positive, things to talk about."

Gwen looked at him with wide eyes and lifted her chin. They were so close, just a few more inches and their lips would meet. But the door behind them opened and Matilda breezed outside. Gwen jumped backward and Albert's hand fell back to his side.

"There you are." Matilda sounded exasperated as she hurried up to them. "If this plan is going to work, you two need to be seen inside together."

Oh yes, the plan. They'd veered pretty far off the original target. "Perhaps you should take a moment to fill me in on this plan of yours."

Gwen shook her head. "Really, I think it's better if you don't know the details. That way, if things go wrong, you can honestly say you had no idea what was going on."

"Then how will I know what to do?"

"All you have to do is stay with me, enjoy the party and dance." She held out her hand. "Can you do that?"

He reached out and took her hand. Oh, yes, he could do that all night long.

More than once that night, Gwen wished there was no plan. She wished that all she had to focus on was Albert and waltzing with him. But she had to remain alert for when Charles took the bait. Unfortunately, he was being agonizingly slow about the whole thing. He danced with Odette, he mingled and spoke with the other guests, but he stayed in the ballroom. If he was planning to make a grab for the necklace, he showed no sign of it.

It was when Matilda and Jason were dancing, and Gwen and Albert were wandering amongst the crowd, that a huge crash sounded at the refreshment table. Moving as quickly as she could, Gwen hurried over with Albert right behind.

Odette stood by the table, the floor around her littered with broken glass and running red with punch. Some of it had splattered on her yellow gown. A waiter stood close by, his face ashen. Odette looked horrified, but also something else that Gwen couldn't quite place.

"Odette, what happened?" Gwen asked.

"I'm not sure. I came over for a glass of punch, and the waiter turned, and we collided."

"I'm so sorry, miss." He held a towel in his hand but obviously had no idea what to do with it.

"It wasn't the waiter's fault," Odette said.

Matilda and Jason hurried up to join them. "What happened?"

Odette kept talking to no one in particular. "I just didn't notice, and I ran into him. I had no idea."

Gwen had experienced more than her share of clumsy moments. She was familiar with the embarrassment, the desire to disappear, but Odette was acting strangely. The way she wrung her hands, her eyes darting from side to side, she looked almost guilty.

"And then all the cups fell," Odette continued. "Oh, dear, I had no idea they'd be so loud."

She had no idea? As if she'd done it on purpose and was surprised by the results. But why...

Albert and Gwen looked at each other at the same time. "The office," Gwen said.

"What?" Odette's voice filled with panic. "No, please don't leave me. I need to apologize. I…I need you to stay."

Somehow, Charles had convinced Odette to create a diversion so he could get into the office. Gwen didn't know whether to be angry with her or feel sorry for her. But that decision could wait until later. She turned to Jason. "Please stay with Odette and make sure she doesn't leave." Then she, Albert and Matilda took off for the office.

What they found when they got there was a shock. The sapphire-and-diamond necklace sat on Father's desk, just where they'd left it. But the drawers of the desk were open and had clearly been rifled through.

Albert pointed at the necklace. "I take it that was the bait you spoke of."

"Yes," Gwen said. "But he never had any intention of stealing it. He came here knowing exactly what he wanted."

Matilda looked around the room in disbelief. "What could Father have had in his desk that was so important to Charles?"

Gwen shook her head. "I have no idea."

"There's probably one person here who does," Albert said. "I believe it's time to speak to Odette."

From the look on the police chief's face, Albert didn't think he was used to having so many Parkies in his station at the same time. The entire Banks family was there, along with all the Pettibones, as well as Albert and Jason. Odette hadn't stopped crying since they walked in the door, and Mr. Pettibone kept roaring about what an outrage it was. Two officers attempted to divide and conquer, moving Odette in one direction and her family in the other, but her three teenage brothers were making it a difficult task.

Finally, Detective Sutter walked in. He looked around the room, shook his head and approached Albert. "This is quite a circus you brought in with you tonight. Would you care to tell me why I was fetched from my bed at this hour?"

Albert motioned for Gwen to come closer. "I only know part of it. Gwen knows the rest."

The two did their best to keep the story short. When Gwen got to the part about baiting Charles with the necklace, Detective Sutter groaned and rubbed his forehead. Then, when he found out about Odette, he looked over his shoulder at the still-hysterical young woman.

"The more I hear, the less I like this Drexler fellow." He motioned for one of the police officers to come over. "Franklin, I need you to take that crying woman to the interrogation room. And if her father gives you any trouble, you have my permission to let him cool down in the holding cell."

Albert hoped the Butcher wasn't still there.

Detective Sutter turned back to Albert. "I want you and Miss Banks to accompany me. That isn't the way we usually do things, you understand. But that woman is so overwrought, she may need to see a familiar face before she can say anything intelligible."

They followed him down the hall to the room. A moment later, Officer Franklin escorted Odette into the room, quickly closing the door behind him as if she might slip out before he could secure her.

Detective Sutter motioned to one of the chairs. "Miss Pettibone, why don't you sit down and relax?"

She looked at the chair as if it might sprout teeth at any moment and attack her. "No, I can't. I shouldn't be here."

The detective sighed. "Do you understand why you're here?"

"I was clumsy. I ran into a waiter."

"Yes," Sutter said. "You caused quite a commotion. And during that time, someone broke into Mr. Banks's office and stole something from his desk. What do you know about that?"

Odette shook her head wildly. "Please, I just want to go home."

"You're not leaving me any choice, Miss Pettibone." The detective turned away from Odette and spoke to Gwen and Albert. "If either of you have anything to say before we lock her up, go ahead."

Gwen stepped forward as Odette dissolved in a fresh torrent of tears. She put her hands on Odette's shoulders. "Listen to me. I know you didn't want to do anything wrong. Somehow, Charles convinced you to help him. But he stole something from my father, so you need to tell us everything you know."

"I can't go to jail. I can't."

"Then talk to us now." Gwen looked over at the detective. "If she tells us what she knows, will she go to jail?"

Sutter shook his head. "Not unless she had an actual hand in the robbery itself, which I don't believe she did."

Gwen squeezed Odette's shoulder. "See? You have nothing to worry about. Just tell us the truth."

For a second, Albert thought Odette was going to

break into a new round of wailing sobs. Instead, she sucked in a few gasping breaths of air and wiped away her tears.

"Charles promised me that we weren't doing anything wrong. He said that Mr. Banks had something of his and refused to give it back. Charles swore to me that he was only retrieving what already belonged to him."

"Where is Charles now?" Albert asked.

"I don't know." Odette hung her head. "He said he'd come back for me after he found his property and we'd go home. But I don't know where he is."

Gwen handed her a handkerchief. "Why did you go along with his plan?"

Odette dabbed at her eyes and looked at Gwen as if she should already know the answer. "He told me he loved me."

Albert sighed. Not only was Charles a thief, but he didn't care who he hurt to get what he wanted. "You don't know what he stole from Mr. Banks, do you?"

"No." Odette looked miserable. "He never told me what it was. Just that it was important to him."

A knock sounded on the door, then it opened just a crack, just enough to slip a piece of paper through. Detective Sutter took it and quickly read it over.

"Lucky for you, Miss Pettibone, it doesn't matter whether or not you know what he took. Mr. Banks was able to determine what has been stolen. Also, he has no desire to press charges against you. You're free to go."

With a gasp, Odette ran the few steps to the partially open door and pushed through it, almost knocking the officer in the hall off his feet. With a few more declarations of "Sorry, I'm so sorry," she ran back to her family.

Albert turned to the detective. "What was stolen?"

"That's a bit of an odd thing," Sutter said. "It was a business ledger."

"A ledger?" Gwen repeated. "With a diamond necklace sitting right on the desk, he spent all his time stealing a ledger?"

"It must be very important to him," Albert said.

"Indeed it must. Also, I suspect he was on to you and your sister, Miss Banks." The detective shook his finger at her. "I should arrest both of you for trying a stunt like that on your own."

Gwen was smart enough to offer nothing in response except a contrite look.

"What happens next?" Albert asked.

"The hunt for Drexler continues. I've posted officers at the entryways of the park. He was seen by several people leaving your home on foot, so unless he steals a horse or an automobile, it's likely that we have him bottled up."

Gwen chewed on her lip, and Albert could tell the wheels of her mind were already whirring, thinking of where Charles might be and how to apprehend him.

Apparently, Detective Sutter deduced the same thing. "I have a word of admonition for both of you, but especially you, miss." He leveled his finger straight at Gwen. "Drexler is more dangerous than I originally believed. He decided to stay in Tuxedo Park after your father kicked him out, which tells me there's something here he needs. It may be the ledger he stole this evening, or it may be something else. My personal belief is that we haven't seen the last of him. Tomorrow is the Fourth of July Picnic. There will be lots of people milling about in the open, which is a perfect cover for any nefarious plans he might have. But I want you both to keep your noses out of this. No more amateur detective work."

Albert nodded.

"Yes, sir," Gwen agreed.

The detective sighed. "At the same time, keep your guard up. In my opinion, Drexler isn't above revenge."

Albert felt Gwen stiffen beside him. Ignoring convention, he slipped his arm around her shoulder. No one was going to hurt her. She'd arrive at the picnic with her family, and then he'd make sure she was never alone.

If Drexler wanted Gwen, he would have to fight his way through Albert.

Chapter 13

If Charles Drexler hoped to find a place he could skulk around without being noticed, the Fourth of July Picnic wasn't it. From the moment her family arrived, all Gwen had heard was people buzzing about what a cad Drexler was, and about the manhunt to find him.

As they strolled through the park to find a spot closer to the lake, Father observed the crowd. "Is it my imagination or has the presence of law enforcement increased since last year?"

"You're not imagining it," Mother said. "There's twice as many, at least."

Matilda huffed out a sigh. "I'm so tired of police investigations and bad people. All I want to do today is have fun."

Gwen hadn't told any of her family the detective's concern that Charles might seek revenge. If she had, they probably wouldn't have let her out of the house. Now, she wondered if she should tell Matilda. Might Charles be a threat to her? But then Jason Adler bounded up, dressed for motoring and grinning like a boy who just found a bullfrog.

They made their greetings all around, and then Jason turned to Matilda. "My automobile is back in tip-top shape. Would you like to go for a drive?"

Matilda looked past Jason. "Father?"

"Of course. Mr. Adler has proven himself more than trustworthy as of late."

Mother looked at him askance, still unaware that the young man intentionally plowed into her beloved statue. No doubt she wondered just how safe Matilda would be in Jason's motorcar, but she said nothing.

"I'd love to," Matilda said to Jason. Then she hesitated. "But there's someone I want to say hello to first."

Gwen turned in the direction Matilda was looking, and for a split second, she thought her heart stopped.

Albert walked toward them carrying a picnic basket in one hand. And on his other arm was Rachel. Her eyes were wide and her cheeks a pretty pink as she took everything in. Gwen thought that the sight of the two of them together just might be the most beautiful thing she'd ever seen.

As soon as Rachel caught a glimpse of Gwen, she gave a little shriek of excitement and began waving.

Gwen walked to meet them and went straight to Rachel, enveloping her in a hug. "I'm so happy to see you. You look wonderful." She stepped back, holding Rachel at arm's length to look at her. "Your hair is so pretty. Did Albert help you with it?"

Rachel beamed. "Yes, he did. But you should show him how you do it. You're much better."

Gwen laughed. "Well, I've had much more practice than your brother." She looked at Albert, and her heart felt like it might burst. She was so overwhelmed with emotion, she could hardly speak—all she could do was smile.

Albert smiled back. "It's good to see you, too."

Father cleared his throat. "If you young people will excuse us, Mrs. Banks and I will put down our blanket and enjoy the view."

As her parents moved away, Matilda said, "Rachel, Jason just offered to take me for a drive in his motorcar. Would you like to join us?"

Rachel looked expectantly at Albert, while Gwen waited to see if he would trust his sister in someone else's care.

Finally, Albert nodded. "Yes, you may. But you have to stay with Matilda and Jason and follow their rules. Do you understand?"

"Oh, yes. Stay with Matilda and Jason. Follow their rules." She clapped her hands, then kissed Albert on the cheek. "Thank you!"

As the three walked away, Albert shook his head. "I don't know if I'm doing the right thing or not. But this is the happiest she's been in years."

"You're being very brave," Gwen said. "I'm proud of you."

Embarrassment crept across Albert's features, and he deftly changed the subject. "It looks like Detective Sutter was serious about his concerns over Drexler."

Gwen nodded. "Yes. There are so many police officers."

"Not only that, but the detective's here."

"He is? Where?"

"Over there. By the big tree."

A man stood under the shade of a huge oak, dressed appropriately for a day in the park. Having never seen Detective Sutter in anything but a suit, it took a moment for her to recognize him.

"I don't know if that should make me feel safer or worry me a bit," Gwen said.

"Oh, you should feel safe. No matter how many police officers and detectives are here, Drexler would have to get through me to get to you. Which will never happen."

Gwen grinned up at him. "In that case, I suggest we enjoy our day."

"A capital idea. What would you like to do?"

"Do you even need to ask? To the archery range."

"I see." Albert nodded slowly. "You've missed several lessons. Are you sure you're up for it? You might be a bit rusty."

Gwen bristled with mock pride. "I'll have you know, sir, I'm just as good now as I was a week ago." Which wasn't spectacularly good, but they both knew that.

"Well, then, let's go."

When they reached the archery range, it was busier than usual. "I'm surprised to see so many people here," Gwen said.

Albert scratched the back of his neck. "I've been told that my notoriety has sparked something of an interest in the sport of archery. It certainly is strange what inspires people."

Gwen couldn't come up with a counterpoint to that. "Oh, dear. You didn't bring your equipment, did you?"

He shook his head. "I didn't think I'd need it. But I still have friends here. Let's go to the equipment shed and get what we need."

"I'm afraid if I leave this spot, someone else will take it, and then we might never get a target."

Albert frowned. "I'm not leaving you alone."

Now he was just being silly. "I'll be perfectly fine. Look, I'm surrounded by people. No one can get to me here."

"No."

Gwen sighed. She really hadn't wanted to say this. "Truth be told, my foot is giving me quite a lot of trouble today. I'd rather not walk any further than I have to."

Albert's face softened. He obviously understood, but was fighting the idea of leaving her alone to fend for herself. Only there was nothing for her to fend off. Charles wouldn't show his face around this many well-armed men and women.

"I'll be fine. I promise."

Finally, he gave in. "All right. I'll be five minutes. I'm going to run over, grab the equipment and come back. And you're not to move from this spot. Do you understand?"

He spoke to her the same way he'd spoken to Rachel. Gwen held back a smile. "Yes, I do."

"All right."

Gwen watched him sprint away to the small building where the bows, arrows and other archery equipment were kept. His movements were so fluid. It was a shame she'd never be able to run with him like that.

A tug on her skirt pulled her from her reverie. She looked down and saw a young boy of about six looking up at her

"Are you Miss Banks?"

"I am."

"Good." He closed his eyes tight as if trying to make a wish or remember something. Then he looked back at her. "Your sister's been in an accident. The car went in the lake. Follow me."

Fear clutched Gwen's heart. "Who told you to come get me?"

The boy didn't answer. He just repeated what he'd said before. "Your sister's been in an accident. The car is in the lake. Follow me."

Then he ran off the archery range.

Gwen didn't know what to do. This could be a ploy to lure her away, but it also could be true. She couldn't take the chance that Matilda had been in an accident and do nothing about it.

"Wait!"

Ignoring the pain in her foot, she ran after the boy, catching sight of him just before he dashed into the foliage at the edge of the range. Every fiber of her being told her this was a bad idea, but there was that one thought that outweighed everything else.

If Matilda is in trouble, I have to help her.

So she ran. She ran through the bramble and past tree branches that pulled at her clothes and hit her face. She ran after the boy toward the lake, each step bringing more pain, more worry. Until finally, when a hand shot out and grabbed her arm, yanking her from her feet, she was almost relieved. And when the sweet-smelling rag covered her mouth and nose, one final thought filled her head.

At least Matilda's all right.

* * *

Someone was moaning. As she tried to move one achy limb and then another, Gwen realized the moans were coming from her.

She opened her eyes slowly. She was sitting on the ground, surrounded by trees. From the bite of bark on her back, she realized she must be leaning against one. Slowly, memories returned. She'd been chasing a boy. He'd told her that Matilda was in trouble. But Matilda was fine. Gwen was the one in trouble.

Charles stood several feet away from her, looking down with distain.

"You just couldn't leave it alone," he said. "All you had to do was go along with it, and everything would have been fine. But you don't know your place."

Her head ached from whatever he'd used to knock her out. It made clear thought difficult. "What are you talking about?"

"If you'd just accepted me as your beau, none of this would have been necessary." He began pacing, as if working out the justification in his own mind. "The robberies, the lies, none of it would have happened if not for you."

Righteous indignation was quickly sweeping the cobwebs from Gwen's mind, and thoughts were coalescing. "You and I never were and never would be a match. How could my refusal to marry you result in all this criminal activity?"

"You don't understand." He raked his fingers through his hair. "None of you understand."

"No, I don't. But if you explain it, maybe I can help."

Charles sneered. "The time for help is over. But if you want to know why, I'll tell you."

Truly, Gwen just wanted to keep him talking. Albert would be looking for her. Any number of people on the archery range would have seen her chase the little boy. They would tell him what they saw. And judging from the trees and plants surrounding them, Charles hadn't taken her very far. If she could keep him occupied, it would give Albert a chance to find her.

"Please, Charles. Please tell me."

"I have debts. A lot of them."

"Lots of people owe money." She tried to sound sweet and understanding, the way Charles expected a woman to sound. "Those things can be worked out."

He laughed in a hard, angry way. "Not with these people. They don't take kindly to late payments."

"I see." Gwen could think of only one possibility that would cause such a reaction. "These are gambling debts, aren't they?"

His glare was answer enough. The facts were coming together in Gwen's head. So Charles had a gambling problem. He had lost a great deal of money and now owed some very bad people.

"But what does this have to do with my father?"

Charles paced faster. "I borrowed money from the company. I thought if I could leverage it, then I could pay everybody and no one would be the wiser."

So he embezzled money and placed bigger, riskier bets in order to win enough money to pay everyone. The man was totally delusional.

"It didn't work, did it?"

"Of course it didn't work," Charles yelled. "If it had, I wouldn't be here talking to you."

A faint rustle off to the left caught Gwen's ear. It wasn't a sound that would be made by an animal that frequented these woods. It would come from something bigger and heavier. Something like a man. *Albert*. She had to keep Charles talking.

"So you curried favor with my father and secured an invitation to our home."

"Yes, that did work out just as I'd hoped. But then I met you, and you were so difficult."

Of course, she'd given him no reason to believe he could win her over. But Matilda had. "I don't understand why you didn't focus your attentions on Matilda instead of me. That still would have accomplished your purpose."

"No." He shook his head. "It had to be the eldest daughter, or else the plan failed."

It took a moment for the implication of that to sink in. As the eldest daughter, Gwen would be in charge of their parents' estate if anything happened to them. Her stomach flipped and grew sour.

"Then I realized this community is full of rich, needy women." He continued his ramblings. "So I changed my focus. And I found I could pick up a few baubles here and there. But it's not enough."

A twig snapped. Charles stopped walking and looked around.

"What about the ledger?" Gwen brought his attention back to her. "Why did you steal that?"

"He brought it home with him from work. Said it had important client information in it. I thought I could use it somehow, but he's got it written in some bizarre code that only he understands."

That explained most of it. Except for what he was doing with her now. "Charles, why did you bring me here? How will this help?"

He looked at her like she was daft. "You're my hostage. Your father gives me the money I need and lets me go on my way, and he'll get you back." His voice rose until it was high and brittle. "I'm desperate. They're going to kill me."

How much money had Charles gambled away? His plan was ridiculous, but his grip on reality seemed to be slipping by the second.

Maybe, if she reasoned with him, she could get out of this. "Charles, there has to be another way. If we could just talk—"

"No, talking won't help. I'm done talking."

He rushed at her, grabbed her arm and hauled her up. She screamed. Behind her, someone burst through the trees.

"It's over, Drexler."

Detective Sutter.

Charles tightened his arm around Gwen's neck, holding her back firmly against his side. "It's not over until I say so. Unless you want me to finish her off now, I suggest you put down that gun."

"You know I can't do that. Let's just talk this through."

"No!" Charles screamed at the detective.

Gwen shut her eyes. *Please Lord, help me.*

From behind Charles came the sound of a wild turkey. Gwen's eyes flew open. *Albert.* It was him.

A moment later the whistle of an arrow split the air and a howl came from Charles as the tip sank into his shoulder. He loosened his grip on Gwen enough for her to drop to her knees and escape his grasp. Sutter ran forward and knocked Drexler to the ground.

Gwen tried to crawl away, but strong hands wrapped

around her upper arms and lifted her to her feet. She looked up and almost cried with happiness.

"Albert. You saved me."

Sutter had Charles facedown on the ground, a knee firmly in the small of his back as he handcuffed the man.

It was over.

"Thank you, Detective." Gwen looked back up at Albert, the only man she had eyes for. "I don't think I can walk right now. Would you please help me?"

Without a second thought, he scooped her up into his arms, and they followed the detective and his prisoner back to the archery range.

After all the explanations had been made, and the police had gotten the information they needed, it had taken a great deal of talking to convince Father that the family should stay at the picnic. He was determined to take Gwen back home and tuck her into bed. In the end, Mother had become the voice of reason.

"The girl needs her rest," Father said.

"The *woman* has been through an ordeal, and now she needs to have a bit of fun," Mother countered. "Besides, Gwen is old enough to make up her own mind."

Father could find no argument against that.

Thankfully, Rachel had been enjoying an auto ride with Jason and Matilda, and had no idea what transpired with Charles. When they returned, Rachel promptly fell asleep on the picnic blanket while Albert filled in the others.

"That's remarkable," Jason said. "How were you able to find them?"

"I knew she'd followed the boy into the woods. After

that, it's really thanks to Gwen." He smiled at her. "She taught me about tracking. And Gwen has a unique gait, so I was able to follow her."

A unique gait. What a beautiful way to describe her limp. "And then, he made the sound of a wild turkey to let me know he was out there."

Albert squeezed her shoulder. "I wasn't sure if you'd realize it was me."

"How did you know?" Matilda asked.

"I'd told Albert the story of how wild turkeys had been released into the woods for the huntsmen, but the turkeys didn't stay around. There are none in these woods anymore. He knew I'd know that."

Jason shook his head. "You two are meant for each other, that's for sure. You're a hero now, Albert, so I dare anyone to trouble you about your class."

Matilda wrapped her fingers around Jason's arm. "With that, I think we'll give you two some privacy." She pulled Jason away with very little trouble.

Albert laughed. "You know, when I first met Mr. Adler, I thought him something of a buffoon, but he's really quite perceptive."

"I'd have to agree," Gwen said.

Albert grew serious. "I have something to ask you."

She could only force out one word. "Yes?"

"Gwen, I—"

"Excuse me!"

A booming voice cut off the question. A short, stocky man with a walking stick approached. Gwen remembered him from the Ashford party. It was Mr. Winchester.

"Forgive me for interrupting you young people. I'm Wallace Winchester." He held out his hand.

Albert shook it heartily. "Of course. We've met once before. So good to see you again. This is Miss Gwendolyn Banks."

"Miss Banks, a pleasure. So sorry to hear about the business going on lately."

Gwen smiled her thanks. "Yes, but I'm doing quite well now. The true criminal has been captured, and Mr. Taylor's good name has been restored."

Mr. Winchester grinned. "More than just restored. From what I hear, Mr. Taylor is a hero who saved the day with a bow and arrow. Which is what I wanted to talk to him about." He turned to Albert. "I heard you lost your sponsors for the competition. Terribly shortsighted of them, to my mind. But you are just the kind of man I want representing the Winchester Archery Company."

Gwen's heart soared.

Albert was struck nearly speechless. "Mr. Winchester, that's wonderful. Thank you."

Mr. Winchester slapped Albert's back. "Fabulous. We can discuss the details tomorrow. For now, I say we all should enjoy this most festive picnic."

Without waiting for a response, the man was off, calling to another person about whether or not they planned to participate in the three-legged race.

Gwen laughed. "It's going to take some energy to keep up with him."

"Oh, no. If I can keep up with you, I can keep up with anybody. Which reminds me." He took her hand. "I was going to ask you a question."

"Yes. You were."

"I wondered, how would you feel about being courted by someone below your station?"

Gwen played along, making a face as though she

were considering it. "That depends. Does he have prospects?"

"Yes, tons. He works hard. He's honest and loyal. And there's talk that he might be participating in the games."

"That sounds very promising."

"You should know, he has a sister. She's a handful, but he loves her. She'll probably always need to live with him. Would you be able to deal with that?"

"Oh, yes. I would expect nothing else." Suddenly, Gwen couldn't stand the game any longer. "Albert, I love you."

A smile lit his face. "I love you, beautiful Gwen. And although we've only known each other a short time, I intend to ask your father for your hand."

"That makes me very happy, indeed."

They looked into each other's eyes, content with everything they saw there.

"I want to kiss you," Albert said, "but I don't think this is the right time or place."

"I agree. We'll know when it's right." She leaned closer and lowered her voice. "But I do hope it's soon."

He laughed. "You can count on that."

They enjoyed the rest of the afternoon. Finally, when the sun went down and people were gathering for the grand finale of the evening, they excused themselves and took a walk away from the crowd. Finally, standing at the edge of the lake, surrounded by God's creation, and under a sky filled with the moon, the stars and fireworks bursting in a riot of colors, Gwendolyn Banks received her first kiss from Albert Taylor, the Archer of Tuxedo Park, and the man who'd hit the target of her heart.

Epilogue

For the first time ever, Gwen was concerned about her dress as she walked through the woods. She gathered the skirt together, holding up the hem to keep it from dragging through the dirt and leaves.

"I love you, Gwenie, but I will never understand why we had to come to this place, today of all days."

Gwen looked over her shoulder and smiled. Matilda held her skirts even higher and practically tiptoed her way along, her head turning left, right and left again as though she was afraid some vicious animal would spring out of the trees and attack her. Or worse, dirty her lovely gown.

"This is a very special place to both Albert and me,"

Gwen said. "I can think of no better spot for our wedding."

Behind Matilda, Rachel skipped and frolicked, taking time to examine the plants she saw along the way. She dropped to her knees in the dirt, paying no mind to her dress whatsoever. "Gwen, look at this beautiful fern."

Gwen stopped and nodded in approval. Three weeks ago, Rachel hadn't known a fern from a dandelion. But she'd started accompanying Gwen on her nature walks and had proven to be quite an adept student. In fact, now that Rachel was no longer confined to the house, she was blossoming in a number of ways.

"Yes, it's a beautiful plant," Gwen said. "We'll come back another day to catalog it. But for now, we need to be going. Albert is waiting."

"Ooh, that's right. This is the day you become my sister!" Rachel popped to her feet and ran ahead, passing Matilda and Gwen.

"Should we stop her?" Matilda asked the question even as she suspiciously eyed a shadowy clump of foliage.

Gwen shook her head. "No. We've been out here a number of times. She knows the way."

Bringing up the rear, Mother and Father walked in contented silence. Like most parents, they wanted to know their child would be happy, and Gwen knew they had worried about her over the years. No doubt they'd had times when they thought this day would never come.

Truth be told, Gwen still had moments of amazement herself. Albert's courtship of her could certainly be dubbed a whirlwind, but when he'd gotten the job offer from Mr. Winchester, they'd had to move quickly. In a week's time, Albert would be moving to Pennsylvania, and there was no way Gwen would let him go without her. Still, there were times when she thought perhaps she was experiencing a very long, very detailed dream, and any moment she would awake to find her life as ordered and predictable as it had always been.

A tug on her dress brought her mind back to the present. The lace of her puffed sleeve had caught on the pointed end of a tree branch. Carefully, she pulled the material away and then turned herself sideways to maneuver safely down the path. Her dress was modest by almost anyone's standards, but to Gwen, it was the stuff dreams were made of. Yards of fine ecru lace topped a satin bodice and skirt of the same color. There was no train to speak of, given the bride's proclivity for tripping on excessive fabric. Instead, the hem was trimmed with dozens of tiny, deep red, satin rosettes.

"How much farther?" Matilda's good nature was being tested, and now she was coming close to whining.

"Have I told you today how beautiful you look?" Gwen asked.

As always, Matilda was lovely. Her dress was pale pink, the perfect complement to her creamy complexion and flaxen hair. Not to mention the blush in her cheeks that had come from their walk through the woods.

Matilda huffed out a sigh. "Thank you for the compliment. But you didn't answer my question. Are we almost there?"

"As a matter of fact, we are." Gwen pointed to the left. "It's just on the other side of this tree."

"Stop right there, young lady," Father called out, bringing the sisters to a halt.

Gwen frowned. "Is something wrong?"

Father looked stern. "I'll say there is. You can't let your groom see you before I walk you down the aisle."

"There is no aisle," Matilda grumbled.

Father shot her a look. "Before I walk you down the path, then. Mother, you and Matilda please go ahead. Let everyone know we're ready."

When they were alone, Father looked down at Gwen, his expression softening. "My dear girl, I am so proud of you."

Gwen's cheeks grew hot, and a smile sprung to her lips. "Thank you, Father. I'm very happy."

"Yes, I can see that. Albert is exactly the kind of man I should have picked for you, had I been paying attention to what was right in front of my face."

"That's all behind us now," Gwen said.

"Right you are. Everything has worked out the way it was supposed to."

Indeed, it had. The experience with Charles Drexler had been maddening, but in the end, it had opened a dialogue between Gwen and her father, bringing them closer than they'd been before. As usual, God had taken a bad situation and created something good from it.

The sound of a wild turkey cut through the trees, and Gwen laughed out loud. "I do believe that's Albert's signal."

Father shook his head. "I may never understand you young people." He crooked his arm and pointed his elbow in her direction. "Are you ready?"

Gwen slid her hand through his arm. "Absolutely."

Albert's tie was much too tight. It was the only explanation as to why he couldn't draw in a decent breath.

Beside him, Jason Adler stood with his hands clasped behind his back. "Are you all right?"

"Of course," Albert said. "Why do you ask?"

Jason leaned closer. "You look a little pale."

That just proved his thought. The tie was constricting the blood flow. He tugged on the knot and swallowed hard. "Everything is fine."

"Good." Jason slapped him on the back.

Albert shook his head, pondering not for the first time the strange series of events that had brought them to this place. Jason had proven himself to be a loyal and true friend. To everyone's relief, Matilda had also seen the young man's character and had allowed him to court her. So it was that a Parkie was standing as the best man for a villager.

He was about to say something profound to his friend when Rachel broke through the trees. A month ago, he wouldn't have imagined she could handle a walk through the village on her own, let alone the woods, but there she was, smiling with joy.

She ran up to him, her bouquet clutched in one hand. "They're coming."

His heart jumped. Matilda and Mrs. Banks approached. The minister told everyone where to stand, and then he looked at Albert. "All we're missing now is the bride."

Albert nodded. "Leave that to me."

He cupped his hands around his mouth and made the sound he believed replicated the call of a wild turkey. The minister and Mrs. Banks looked slightly shocked, but Matilda and Rachel simply laughed.

"Trust me," Albert said. "Gwen will know what that means."

She didn't disappoint him. A moment later she appeared, led through the trees by her father. Gwen was a vision in satin and lace, holding a simple bouquet of wildflowers in front of her. His breath caught in his chest, and this time, he couldn't blame the tie. Gwen took his breath away, it was as simple as that.

Mr. Banks stopped beside Albert. After giving his daughter a kiss on the cheek, he took her hand from his arm and held it out to Albert. "Take good care of her, son."

He tucked her hand into the crook of his arm. "You have my word, sir."

Mr. Banks stepped away and joined his wife. Then Gwen looked up at Albert, her face glowing with love and trust, and for a moment, Albert thought his heart might burst.

There in the woods, standing before their family and friends, they said their vows in the shade of the pawpaw tree. *Their* tree, where they had met just two short months earlier. And when the minister proclaimed, "You may kiss the bride," Albert could have sworn the birds joined in with the cheers and shouts from the people around them.

Albert hugged his bride to his side and turned to face the small group. Gwen gasped, and for a moment, he was afraid she had caught her foot on an exposed root.

"What's wrong?"

Gwen shook her head. Her voice was low as she pointed at Rachel. "Look."

Rachel stood still as a statue, holding her bouquet in both her hands. And sitting atop the flowers, moving its wings very slowly, was a butterfly.

Albert couldn't believe it. "That's not what I think it is, is it?"

"Yes." Gwen laughed, even as a tear rolled down her cheek. "It's a zebra swallowtail. After all that time chasing it, it finally came to me."

Rachel looked at her new sister-in-law, her eyes wide with amazement. "Look, Gwen. I caught a butterfly."

"Yes you did, *leibling*." Gwen nodded. "But we must let it fly away. It has many adventures ahead of it, I'm sure."

"Just as we do." Albert hugged her again, certain that with her by his side, his life would always be filled with wonder and love.

* * * * *

REQUEST YOUR FREE BOOKS!

2 FREE INSPIRATIONAL NOVELS
PLUS 2
FREE
MYSTERY GIFTS

Love Inspired®

YES! Please send me 2 FREE Love Inspired® novels and my 2 FREE mystery gifts (gifts are worth about $10). After receiving them, if I don't wish to receive any more books, I can return the shipping statement marked "cancel." If I don't cancel, I will receive 6 brand-new novels every month and be billed just $4.99 per book in the U.S. or $5.49 per book in Canada. That's a saving of at least 17% off the cover price. It's quite a bargain! Shipping and handling is just 50¢ per book in the U.S. and 75¢ per book in Canada.* I understand that accepting the 2 free books and gifts places me under no obligation to buy anything. I can always return a shipment and cancel at any time. Even if I never buy another book, the two free books and gifts are mine to keep forever.   105/305 IDN GH5P

Name	(PLEASE PRINT)

Address	Apt. #

City	State/Prov.	Zip/Postal Code

Signature (if under 18, a parent or guardian must sign)

Mail to the **Reader Service:**
IN U.S.A.: P.O. Box 1867, Buffalo, NY 14240-1867
IN CANADA: P.O. Box 609, Fort Erie, Ontario L2A 5X3

**Are you a subscriber to Love Inspired® books
and want to receive the larger-print edition?
Call 1-800-873-8635 or visit www.ReaderService.com.**

* Terms and prices subject to change without notice. Prices do not include applicable taxes. Sales tax applicable in N.Y. Canadian residents will be charged applicable taxes. Offer not valid in Quebec. This offer is limited to one order per household. Not valid for current subscribers to Love Inspired books. All orders subject to credit approval. Credit or debit balances in a customer's account(s) may be offset by any other outstanding balance owed by or to the customer. Please allow 4 to 6 weeks for delivery. Offer available while quantities last.

Your Privacy—The Reader Service is committed to protecting your privacy. Our Privacy Policy is available online at www.ReaderService.com or upon request from the Reader Service.

We make a portion of our mailing list available to reputable third parties that offer products we believe may interest you. If you prefer that we not exchange your name with third parties, or if you wish to clarify or modify your communication preferences, please visit us at www.ReaderService.com/consumerschoice or write to us at Reader Service Preference Service, P.O. Box 9062, Buffalo, NY 14240-9062. Include your complete name and address.

REQUEST YOUR FREE BOOKS!

2 FREE INSPIRATIONAL NOVELS
PLUS 2 *FREE* MYSTERY GIFTS

Love Inspired® HISTORICAL

YES! Please send me 2 FREE Love Inspired® Historical novels and my 2 FREE mystery gifts (gifts are worth about $10). After receiving them, if I don't wish to receive any more books, I can return the shipping statement marked "cancel." If I don't cancel, I will receive 4 brand-new novels every month and be billed just $4.99 per book in the U.S. or $5.49 per book in Canada. That's a saving of at least 17% off the cover price. It's quite a bargain! Shipping and handling is just 50¢ per book in the U.S. and 75¢ per book in Canada.* I understand that accepting the 2 free books and gifts places me under no obligation to buy anything. I can always return a shipment and cancel at any time. Even if I never buy another book, the two free books and gifts are mine to keep forever.

102/302 IDN GH6Z

Name	(PLEASE PRINT)
Address	Apt. #
City	State/Prov.	Zip/Postal Code

Signature (if under 18, a parent or guardian must sign)

Mail to the **Reader Service:**
IN U.S.A.: P.O. Box 1867, Buffalo, NY 14240-1867
IN CANADA: P.O. Box 609, Fort Erie, Ontario L2A 5X3

Want to try two free books from another series?
Call 1-800-873-8635 or visit www.ReaderService.com.

* Terms and prices subject to change without notice. Prices do not include applicable taxes. Sales tax applicable in N.Y. Canadian residents will be charged applicable taxes. Offer not valid in Quebec. This offer is limited to one order per household. Not valid for current subscribers to Love Inspired Historical books. All orders subject to credit approval. Credit or debit balances in a customer's account(s) may be offset by any other outstanding balance owed by or to the customer. Please allow 4 to 6 weeks for delivery. Offer available while quantities last.

Your Privacy—The Reader Service is committed to protecting your privacy. Our Privacy Policy is available online at www.ReaderService.com or upon request from the Reader Service.

We make a portion of our mailing list available to reputable third parties that offer products we believe may interest you. If you prefer that we not exchange your name with third parties, or if you wish to clarify or modify your communication preferences, please visit us at www.ReaderService.com/consumerschoice or write to us at Reader Service Preference Service, P.O. Box 9062, Buffalo, NY 14240-9062. Include your complete name and address.

LIH15